To Jordan . . .

Enjoy!

Highland Justice

Doug Godsman

ISBN-13: 978-1981186396

ISBN-10: 1981186395

Dedication

To Jennifer and Neil

My children

Of whom I am inordinately proud

To Phyllis

With thanks for her

Support, Encouragement and

Never-ending belief that I would finish!

And

To second-sons everywhere.

Part 1

"Farewell to the Highlands,

farewell to the north"

"Farewell to the Highlands"

Robert Burns

Chapter 1

Emigrating to America! California!

Bella Gordon perched herself on the granite wall outside the family's wee cottage and enjoyed a last cup of tea. The cleaning was finished, the packing also, and she could finally look forward to the momentous journey to California they would embark upon tomorrow. *California!*

Big brother George plopped down beside her, enjoying the unusually warm Scottish September sun.

"Weel, Sis, off on the big adventure tomorrow, eh?"

"Aye, George, up bright and early for the morning train. Don't sleep in now, you hear?!"

"No chance, Bella, no wi' Faither sheep-dogging us! We'll be up and aboot lang before we need to be!" They both laughed. Being late for anything represented a sin in Harry Gordon's eyes; being late for the train starting the family's journey to America was unthinkable.

"Bella," George continued, "tell the truth now. What did you imagine when Faither told us we were off to join Uncle Jack in California?"

"He floored me! I had no idea Mum and Dad were even thinking of it, although with Da losing his job when the distillery closed, I sensed there would be changes."

George nodded in agreement. Bella continued: "But America! If they had wanderlust in their hearts, they hid it well! I didn't suppose they had it in them to make such a move. They fair amazed me."

"But …?" George left the question hanging like a hawk over a field mouse.

"Well, then I got angry. I had finished my last year at The Albyn School and wanted to become a tutor somewhere near here and wasn't happy about my plans being thrown into disarray. But as time passed, and I got used to the idea, I got more and more excited. America! California! I canna believe it!" Bella's practical side peeked through. "Uncle Jack must be doing well there to pay for our fares. The tickets for the ship are fifteen pounds each; then there's the train fare to California!"

"Aye, his letters say it's hard work out there but you can mak somethin' o' yerself, too. And there's none o' us afraid o' a wee bit of work!"

Their Ma, Fiona Gordon, came out of the cottage and went to visit a neighbor, happy that her work was done. This left her Da, Harry, at a loose end. And he knew exactly what to do about that.

#

The old wooden box had sat on the sunny side of the front doorstep for as long as Bella could remember. The many bums gracing it had smoothed it to the touch and the wild Scottish weather had faded it to a deep sepia. But, if you took a close look, you could still see the faint red writing painted on the side in fine flowing script.

Dalmurdo Distillery

Ballboyne, Scotland

Harry Gordon had made the box years ago. He had been a cooper, crafting barrels and crates from local oak for the distillery before it closed down in mid-1904. This was a strong, solid box, the dado joints tight and sturdy as befitted its original purpose in life. After all, you couldn't have bottles of whisky breaking free and rolling around! But over the years, this whisky crate had become Harry's preserve. He straddled it when he took to playing.

Harry was a fiddler. Now, he didn't support his family by fiddling—no, the music was his love, his passion, his fever. Sometimes he made a bob or two, but peace and contentment were his primary reward, rare commodities in rural Scotland.

Bella watched her father scrape his playing pew away from the cottage wall. As usual, it not being Sunday, he wore a grey woolen work shirt with no collar and faded black woven trousers held up by black galluses. The polish on his boots resembled a mirror, his cap boasted five shades of grey, sewn from several bolts of leftover cloth. A beanpole of a man with a monk's fringe of graying hair, Harry had a quizzical crease between his bright blues, suggesting he never trusted what they saw. Between the eyes was a purple nose familiar with the bottom of too many whisky glasses.

Bella herself appeared tall for a girl. Girl? A seventeen-year-old woman, more likely. Five feet eight inches of intelligence and vivacious curiosity. Her physical attributes were stunning, but her personality matched her form and this made her so attractive. Especially as she didn't realize her beauty.

Harry took his fiddle out of its time-worn leather case and smiled at her. Soon, the soothing tune of a Scottish ballad filled the evening air. All would be well.

Harry's music drew the villagers of Ballboyne to the spontaneous farewell party. Fellow musicians appeared and added their harmonies. First came the accordion player, Billy 'No-Chin' Anderson and his wife Bessie, another fiddler. Big Roy Colquhoun showed up, sweating and swearing as he hauled his double bass through the village, vowing yet again to learn the piccolo. A few of the military lads dribbled in from the barracks, one fife at a time, along with a drummer or two. Mary MacKay, the greengrocer's wife, got roped in, not that she resisted too much, and was soon banging away on the piano through the open window of the Kings Arms across the road. Jamie Anderson dug out his squeezebox; even old Neil Campbell, the blind fluteplayer, stumbled over from his cottage to sit in with the impromptu band. The resulting rampaging music sounded fine but it forever teetered on the brink of chaos, so Dr. Mutch, the minister, stepped in to select the music and to conduct. A right rare wee ceilidh soon broke out.

Bella couldn't decide whether to be happy or sad, excited or nervous. At last, she surrendered, letting herself yield to the music and blotting out thoughts of tomorrow and the momentous journey her family had planned. Dr. Mutch switched to dance music causing an outbreak of jigs, strathspeys and reels on the cobblestones of Bridge Street. Bella joined in with laughter in her eyes and wings on her feet. The dancers swirled and swung, to and fro, hither and yon, the Dashing White Sergeant, an Eightsome Reel, the Gay Gordons. Bella danced until she ran out of breath then sat back down on the stone wall, catching her wind and watching while new blood took to the cobblestone stage.

Her mother Fiona came and sat with her, still full of energy despite the last-minute packing and cleaning. Short, plump and grey at 40, the lines on her face came from laughter, not worry. The two women enjoyed the antics of the young children dancing as they tried to follow the steps of their elders, but slipping and sliding on the setts. The middle children divided into the boy-girl camps, the girls standing on one side, arms crossed, watching as the boys wrestled to show their 'manliness', the ancient tribal rite not yet lost.

Big brother George settled beside them, sweating like a shoat, jacket off, tie half round his neck, shirttail flapping in the breeze. Bella looked at him with a fond eye. She tried to bring order to his hair, reaching up and combing her fingers through his copper tangle. He grinned at her as she laughed and surrendered, his jumbled mass winning once again. Big, good natured, strong and honest to a fault, his five years as infantryman in the Black Watch had turned the shy, callow youth with the squashed-up nose and archipelago of freckles into a confident, attractive young man.

Mrs. McPhee, the banker's wife, made her way through the dancers, disapproval vibrating from every fiber of her being.

"Good day, Mrs. McPhee, a fine evening!" sang Fiona.

"Yes, if you like it humid." Mrs. McPhee never enjoyed a good mood.

"Nice to see the sun today!" Fiona refused to have her pleasure of the moment squashed.

"Aye, but it'll be stormy for your little trip tomorrow!" Mrs. McPhee had passed the family by now and this last comment, spat over her shoulder, brooked no reply.

"Blast!" said Fiona, "Once, just once, I'd liked to have had the last word with her!" She left to catch another friend who seemed to be searching for her.

Bella turned to George to continue their discussion about America when she heard horses approaching. The peak of the hump-backed bridge stopped her from seeing who the impending riders were right away, but then, in slow motion, she saw a hat, then a head, then a jacket until a whole young man bobbed up out of the stonework, one of a party of four.

"Whose horse is that out in front?" she asked George. She stood to get a closer look at the rider. Her tone changed from idle curiosity to vital fascination. "And who's the man riding him?"

George didn't like where this was going. The horsemen were level with them now and the lead rider seemed to take a burning interest in his sister, in fact, he almost rode into the gable-end of a neighboring cottage. If it weren't for the quick intervention of a fellow rider, a ghillie by the look of him, the leader would have been tossed off, for sure.

George nodded his head and knuckled his brow to the passing nobility. To his amazement, he noticed from the corner of his eye Bella had done nothing of the sort, no curtsy, no dipping of the eyes, nothing but a bold, brazen even, stare. George, though a hardheaded male, felt the tension between the two, lingering as the horses turned towards the river.

"Thank goodness we're leaving tomorrow," he thought, *"or there would be trouble!*

#

Bella insisted, George tried hard not to say anything encouraging but, well, Bella insisted. "Who was the first rider, George, tell me! And don't say you don't know because it's clear you do! I want to know the name of the man on the lead horse!" She leaned over until her eyes were inches away from George's.

Caught like a rabbit mesmerized by a weasel, George had no choice but to answer.

"Sis, you know him as Sir David of Crachan. But I want you to forget you ever saw him."

"Forget him? Why on earth should I forget him?"

“Because no possible good can come from any interest he may have in you or you in him. The nobility is all alike when it comes to women; they show interest in our class for what’s beneath the skirts. They arrange anything more serious amongst themselves, within the aristocracy.”

“Sir David? I knew of him before I started boarding school. Well, hasn’t he grown up to be a fine specimen of a man! Tell me more.”

George groaned. Obviously, Bella wouldn’t heed his warning. “No, Bella, there’s no point in me telling you more. He’s nobility, he’s older, he’s off-limits to you!”

Bella’s eyebrows met in a ferocious frown. “I don’t care if he’s the Prince of Prussia, tell me what you know!” Her voice had risen many decibels; her face an angry mask. Stamp her feet and the image of a spoilt brat would have been complete.

George looked around in desperation for reinforcements.

Chapter 2

David took his time. He had but one chance. He eased his Lee-Enfield into position on his right shoulder, shut his left eye, adjusted his aim to take into account his calculations for distance, wind, elevation and temperature, cleared his mind, took his final breath, and squeezed the trigger.

#

The long day had started well before the early Scottish dawn.

"Sir David, get out of bed, ye lazy beggar!" Tam McKenzie shook David's leg.

The Honorable Sir David Rennie, second son of Lord Adam Rennie of Crachan, kicked and thrashed his legs to put an end to his torment, or, even better, his tormentor. Any hungover person would have done the same. "Get away from me, Damn your eyes! What the hell are you doing? Good grief, it's not even daylight yet!"

Tam set the candle on the table by the side of the bed, its pale-yellow glow attempting to dispel the gloom, but the sixteen-foot ceilings, Dark furnishings and the even darker draperies swallowed the light long before it got to the extremities of the bedchamber. "All the better for the hunting, Sire!"

"Hunting? What hunting?"

"Don't you remember, Sir David? The last thing you said last night, or, rather, this morning, was 'Let's bag Leviathan!' Your exact words, Sire."

David groaned. He did remember his wish to hunt Leviathan. The massive sixteen-point stag had been the quarry of every local hunter since his appearance on Royal Deeside four years past. But, David reflected, Tam shouldn't hold him responsible for the thoughts, deeds, actions or words occurring during his twenty-first birthday celebrations.

"Coffee!" he croaked.

"Right here, Sire, with a wee bit of the 'hair of the dog' to get you started."

David sat up in his four-poster, pushed the curtains aside, swung his legs round and moaned, holding his head while he waited for the room to stop reeling. "Wipe that grin off your face, blast you! Anyway, how come you haven't got a hangover?"

"Well, Sir David, I didn't participate in five drinking races in a row. You held your own, though, until the last of those pints of McEwan's. I saw Lord Milne's team spike it with something."

David took a cautious sip of his coffee, made a face as the whisky bit, then let out a long sigh as its remedial effects started their magic on his throbbing temples. "Oh yes, now I remember." He groaned again. "Why didn't you stop me?"

"I did, sir, but the damage had already been done. You, ahem, fell asleep soon after."

"Kindly said, Tam. Kindly said" David took another sip of coffee. "I presume the lads are downstairs waiting for me?"

"Aye, they are, sir. I've laid out your clothes and taken the liberty of having sandwiches made for breakfast so you can eat as we ride to Loch Muick." Tam didn't add David's normal menu of kippers, bacon and eggs wouldn't have stayed south of his gullet for long.

David sighed, "Right then. I can't disappoint them. Tell them I'll be ready to go in fifteen minutes. And bring more coffee!"

David dressed for the day of hunting, donning his brown tweed shooting jacket last. He checked himself in the mirror.

Wow! You look as bad as I feel! he mumbled to the apparition staring back at him.

Anyone else would have seen a tousled, healthy young man with carbon black hair and sapphire eyes. He stood a whisker over six feet with a strong, athletic body, thanks to the hard labor he had put in around the estate at his father's insistence. Lord Rennie wanted him to see how the other 99 percent of the world lived and so add nuance and humility to his character. Plenty of David's noble friends carried themselves with arrogance and inflated self-importance and Lord Rennie didn't want David to mimic them. Tam would mutter in rare agreement with the Lord. "Your boarding school mates consider themselves God's gifts to the rest of us! Real strength of character comes not from arrogance, but from justice. We're all Jock Thamson's bairns, Sir David, and don't you forget it!"

It had taken David a long time to realize Tam meant we were all seeds of the same fruit, and pure happenstance and history had made David and his family 'Lords of the Realm'. His comfort in this knowledge and the ease he had about himself attracted both men and women like bees to honey. (Tam would have said "…flies to dead meat!")

David made his way down the wide staircase, grabbed a rain jacket and stepped into the cobbled courtyard at the back of the Castle Crachan, his family's seat for many generations. He breathed deeply, savoring the crisp, morning air, the smell of the horses and their leather tack, all evocative yet sad. He'd miss them.

David tried three times before he successfully climbed onto the back of Haddock, his big black hunter. The rest of the party looked the other way, trying not to smirk.

"All right! Let's go."

David, Tam and two gamekeepers, each with a pack horse in tow, jangled along the driveway, through the gates and along the dark and deserted streets of the perfect wee village, Ballboyne. They clattered over the bridge across the River Dee and on up through the mud of the track to Loch Muick. David's eyes were half-closed for the first part of the journey, but the fresh September air, the coffee, the whisky and the chat of his companions soon roused him into taking an interest in his surroundings.

"Well, Tam, what's the plan for today?"

"The weather's warm, Sire, so the deer are still high on the hills. I spotted several hundred at Dhoulain Corrie, led by Leviathan. The wind's from the east so we'll leave the horses at the Falls of Muick and climb to the West Spur."

David groaned; he didn't fancy a long, energetic stalk, particularly being well below his best form. But he had said he would and so he would, a matter of honor. And Tam's plan made sense. If the deer were still in the Corrie, the natural bowl cut out of the granite hillside by the retreat of an ancient ice cover, the one way to approach unseen and downwind involved coming off the West Spur. Tam was right again.

David mused on Tam. David's father had hired his mentor twenty years past and Tam had grown from military man to gamekeeper or ghillie. Then, over the years, Tam became David's personal aide and bodyguard. Now the young nobleman looked at Tam's broad back and easy seat on his eighteen-hand horse. *Was there anything this man couldn't do?* Tam's time as Sergeant in the Gordon Highlanders, Britain's premier infantry regiment, made him the natural choice to teach David the noble skills of shooting and fishing.

Tam, now in his late forties, still as straight and hard as an oak, boasted a full head of hair revealing a hint of gray at his temple. His muttonchops, wrapping around from his sideburns to his mustache, gave him an irresistible devil-may-care air. He was a handsome man who had never married. "Marriage and soldiering don't mix, David," Tam had explained, avoiding the inconvenient fact he hadn't been a soldier for many years. David knew the rumors suggesting

Tam's bed was seldom cold when he climbed under the covers. A man's man, a vital man, David's teacher, mentor, guide and now friend, despite the class distinction.

It took David and Tam three hours to climb close to the rim of the Corrie. The two ghillies remained below with the horses, waiting for the signal to come and pick up the spoils of the hunt. The sun's rise coincided with the temperature warming to the low sixties, despite the inevitable breeze. David sweated himself clean, clear and sober in the first hour. At last, he began to appreciate his surroundings, the cliffs and crags of the Grampian Mountains to the west and north, painted purple above the tree line by the bell heather, in contrast to the softer, rolling hills to the east. The River Dee embraced the many greens of the valley, curling through the fertile fields and around the golf course. The forests were resplendent with the autumn show of golds and russet counterpoint to the dark green of the conifers.

David appreciated the tranquility most of all. Yes, he heard birds, crows cawing, the vertical flight and song of a lark, the harsh stutter of a grouse that had escaped the previous week's sweep, but these were calls to peace of mind. Nature at its purest. It had a magical, healing quality. He would need it to get through the rest of the week with his emotions intact.

The last hundred yards to the rim of the Corrie required scrambling and crawling through the heather and mud in total silence. Tam eased David's gun case ahead of him. It contained David's rifle, a modified Lee-Enfield sniper's weapon David had learned to use with supreme accuracy under Tam's expert tutelage. With infinite care, the two men peeked round a large clump of heather and scanned the Corrie below them.

Nothing!

"Tam, if you've brought me up here on a fool's errand, I'll have your guts for garters!" David hissed.

"Now, Sir David, don't be too hasty. There's still a lot of places they might be!"

Tam was right; the Corrie stretched a mile across with crevices and ravines and spurs of rock where a multitude of deer might hide. David withdrew his spotting scope from the heavy metal case draped over his chest. Tam did likewise and they swept the Corrie walls searching for any sign of life. It took five minutes but David spotted the does first. They were to the east and below, emerging from a fold in the slopes five hundred yards away. David grabbed Tam's arm and pointed.

"There they are." he whispered, as the herd grew from a few to dozens to hundreds of them. "But where's Leviathan?"

"Wait!" Tam whispered back, "Isn't that him coming now?"

Sure enough, the unmistakable head and antlers preceded the massive body from behind an immense boulder. The two men watched in awe, then panic when Leviathan stopped dead in his tracks and looked straight at them. Both the hunters and the hunted froze like granite statues—unmoving, petrified in all senses of the word. Leviathan lifted his splendid head and bugled, a deep, coughing, harsh sound that captured his harem's attention. He turned and led the herd back away from the hunters, back behind the rocky ridge until they were out of sight.

David dropped back into the heather, beside himself. "How did he know we were here? I should have had my gun ready! What are we going to do? Damn! Damn! Damn!"

"Sir David, it's not the end of the world!"

"But…"

"Sire, there's two things Leviathan can do. He can lead the herd up the ravine and over the rim of the Corrie, or he can stay hidden from sight where he is now. Either way, you have a chance, provided you have a loaded gun in your hand!"

Tam unfastened the buckles on the hunting case as he spoke and drew out the rifle. He'd cleaned it himself yesterDay, nevertheless he inspected it with care. He opened the tin of cartridges and selected one, opened the breech, slipped the bullet home and closed the lever. David kept a close eye on the ridge hiding the herd, hoping they would stay there and allow him to crawl round the rim of the Corrie for a closer and easier shot. But when Leviathan came into view, he now appeared to be some six hundred yards away, leading his herd up the steep eastern slope toward the rim and freedom.

With Tam focused on preparing the gun, David bit his tongue rather than make frivolous remarks such as "Hurry up!" Instead, he studied the wind, both up here and in the Corrie. He estimated the elevation change and the distance before deciding how much he would need to modify his aim.

It was a long shot but David had confidence in his ability. At last, Tam whispered, "Sir David!" and passed the Lee-Enfield to him. David sensed tension building within himself and started the deep breathing exercises Tam had taught him, willing his heart rate to diminish, and soon he felt his mind clear and a cool determination take over. Leviathan halted on top of the ridge, perhaps waiting for his ladies to finish the ascent. One step behind him stood a magnificent doe, maybe the matriarch of the society, a beauty in her own right.

David took his time. He had but one chance. He eased his Lee-Enfield into position on his right shoulder and shut his left eye. He fixed the sight on the deer's heart, inches behind the front leg. He adjusted his aim to take into account his calculations for distance, wind, elevation and temperature, cleared his mind, took his final breath and squeezed the trigger.

The shot rang out, echoing round the Corrie.

"You missed!" Tam couldn't believe it. "You daft gommerel, you didna even wound him! Leviathan's gone!" The rest of the herd scattered, most of them bolting over the ridge.

David smiled. "Look again, Tam."

Tam peered through his scope and spotted a deer down. But it wasn't Leviathan; it was the matriarch. "I don't understand, Sir David!"

"I didn't miss, I killed what I aimed at, the matriarch. I saw Leviathan standing on the ridge, in the prime of life, doing what he does best. And I decided I didn't want killing him to be my last act here."

Tam stared at him in amazement, trying to catch the import of what the younger man had said. At last, he understood what David meant about not shooting Leviathan, but the rest?! What did he mean 'his last act'?

"Come on, Tam, get the lads up here and dress the deer out. Make sure the venison goes to the families on the estate; it's been a rough summer."

#

A tired heckle of hunters shambled down to the bridge. They had worked hard, David and Tam alongside the ghillies. It had still taken hours to clean the matriarch, cut her up into manageable chunks, load them into the saddlebags of the packhorses before descending to Ballboyne. Now the gloaming crept upon them, the magical time between day and night, when the colors become blurred and softened. The sky deepened to a cobalt blue, the few clouds shaded into creams and smudges of violet, the mountains' black shadows lengthened, the wind died down to a calm whisper. Only the songbirds showing signs of increased vigor as they warbled and trilled from the topmost twigs, staging one last territorial aria.

There had been a shower in mid-afternoon and the grey granite cottages of Ballboyne shone and shimmered, the sunset reflecting off the mica embedded in the stone. Substantial were these hundred or so wee homes, sturdy and enduring, with smoke rising from the chimneys over the coal cooking fires. From David's vantage point above the river, he saw the Dee winding around the village like the horseshoe on a smithy's wall, the spire of the Presbyterian Kirk acting as the nail from which the horseshoe hung.

They heard music long before they came to the rise of the bridge.

"Tam, what's going on? It sounds like a sizable event."

"I have no idea, Sir David. I'll find out if you wish!"

"No, let them be. It's been a hard year, what with the miserable weather and the poor harvest. They've earned some relief. We'll take the back path so we don't disturb …." His voice trailed off.

Tam looked round and saw David 's eyes transfixed on the woman standing by the bridge's approach. And for good reason. Tam had never seen a more beautiful girl here in Ballboyne; in fact, he was hard-pressed to remember any woman who might best her. She had the wavy, raven hair from her Celtic forebears and startling grey eyes. Her skin was flawless, too tanned to be fashionable but vibrant and healthy, as was her form, well defined, slim yet strong. Tam judged her to be seventeen and almost too young to realize how attractive she was.

She flashed an impish smile and David was smitten…irrefutably, irrevocably, permanently smitten.

Chapter 3

Lord Adam Rennie's hands trembled in anger and humiliation as he read the police report for the third time.

How could I have been so stupid?

He threw the report onto his desk and stared out of the window at his favorite view. The Castle Cranach parklands, his parklands, were framed by copper beeches with the majestic Grampian Mountains as a backdrop. But that day he saw nothing through his misery.

Damn Tookov!

He'd known ever since he received the report he would need to meet with his two sons, James and David, and confess to the irresponsible investments he'd made but his mind still shied away from the confrontation. David, his youngest, would take it in stride as he did all things. But James, the heir to Lord Rennie's now non-existent fortune, would explode in a wrathful, childish fury. Nonetheless, he needed to call a family council and admit to his disastrous misjudgment.

He sighed, picked up the report and read it once again, hoping to draw a different conclusion but expecting none.

Metropolitan Police Service
New Scotland Yard
London

14th Day of August 1904

Lord Adam Rennie
Cranach Castle
Ballboyne
Aberdeenshire
Scotland

My Lord,

I have completed my investigation into Baron Pyotr Tookov and his merchant bank, currently called Silverlake and Dale Ltd. My findings are summarized below. I have also included the conclusions of the Pinkerton Detective Agency of New York although, of course, I cannot vouch for the accuracy of their work.

Baron Pyotr Tookov is a fraud.

He was born in 1852 in the east end of London as Peter Thomas. The authorities are very familiar with his family, they have been arrested multiple times for minor infractions such as forgery and swindling.

Peter Thomas had higher ambitions and apprenticed to a London Merchant Bank, Jacobi and Jonah, in 1867. In 1882, he started his own investment house, Bernard and Epstein. To all outward appearances, this too operated as a merchant bank but Thomas sold shares in nonexistent companies to greedy investors.

As complaints against him mounted, he shuttered his business, only to reopen it under a different name. This he did five times between 1882 and 1903, his most recent 'bank' is called Silverlake and Dale. It is interesting to note his progression through society as his confidence grew. His most recent adopted persona, 'Baron Pyotr Tookov', is supposedly a noble with a Russian background. Thomas is an excellent mimic which facilitates his movement in such circles.

The Letters of Introduction, which add so much to his credibility, are forgeries, no doubt executed by those in his family.

In 1902, the London Metropolitan Police took over the investigation and pursued

Thomas with vigor. He once again closed his 'business', this time liquidating his assets and fleeing to the United States of America, leaving 423 unhappy investors like yourself.

The rest of this summary is from the Pinkerton Detective Agency.

Baron Pyotr Tookov first appeared on the New York investment scene in January of 1903. His affable manner, his 'nobility' and his apparent capacity to find excellent mining prospects soon gathered a considerable following of, one must say, gullible investors. Complaints didn't surface until February of this year, in part because of the handsome returns his initial investors received, also because he had bribed the appropriate police officials.

His current prospect involves the Evening Star silver mine in Arkansas, with which you are familiar. There is such a mine, making it a different fraud than his usual ploys which have no tangible assets. A recent article in the American Miners

Journal suggests there may be value to this mine which may encourage Tookov to change his methods.

Pressure is mounting on New York's Mayor and Chief of Police to apprehend him. Considering Tookov's bought loyalists within the Police Department, he doubtless knows this and it may require him to relocate again. Chicago or Boston are possible destinations.

It is conceivable Tookov may wish to examine the Evening Star mine to determine its value. However, Arkansas is rough country, and as far from the comforts of New York as possible, so this is considered unlikely.

This concludes the summary report. I have attached the supporting details. Please let me know if I can be of any further assistance to you.

Your obedient servant,

DM Henderson

Inspector

Chapter 4

George spotted his mother coming back after visiting with her neighbor, Maggie Pitcaithly.

"Ma!" He shouted, "Over here!" He waved his hands in emphasis.

"What's the matter, George. Why are you shouting?"

"Ma, you need to talk sense into Bella! She's gone stupid over Sir David!"

George and Bella took it in turns to interrupt each other. Bella downplayed her interest in Sir David while her brother exaggerated a little. Fiona heard them both out, then turned to Bella with a smile and a tinge of regret.

"Bella, for once George is right. David has a good and fair reputation with the staff at Crachan, but the nobility mistreats their servants something fierce; young, impressionable, good-looking ones such as you in particular." Bella colored at the unaccustomed praise.

"So, there's no point getting yourself worked up about him. Anyway, you'll never see him again. I admire your taste, though, he's turned out to be a handsome lad!" Fiona turned to her son. "George, I'm glad you're concerned for your sister and your instincts regarding the upper crust are accurate. There's at least half-a-dozen bairns running around Ballboyne because of young lassies' dalliances with the men from the castles. But we're leaving tomorrow. Keep your eyes open for your sister on the trip, and don't worry so much about Ballboyne. Now, will you dance with your old Mum?" Harry and his 'band' were playing 'Corn Riggs' and Fiona and George disappeared into the crowd.

Bella wished and wondered, needing more information about her knight on a black horse. Ah, here came her friend and cousin, Sheila Anderson.

"Sheila, Sheila, come sit with me!" And the two friends were soon engrossed in Bella's upcoming travels and Sheila's recent romance with Neil Munroe, the apprentice gardener at the Royal's Balmoral Castle.

Bella turned the conversation to the uppermost topic on her mind. "You'll never guess who I just saw!"

"By the color in your cheeks, it must have been someone special! Who was he, pray tell!"

"Sir David of Crachan!"

"Oh, he is special, right enough! A handsome lad, and single too! How did you come to see him?"

Bella told of the horses coming into sight and how Sir David almost rode into the cottage across the way because he stared at her.

Sheila laughed. "That's our David, right enough! He's a most accomplished man, well-traveled, well read. The staff loves him, but he's awfie awkward around women. Mum still works at Castle Crachan and told me Lord Rennie threw Sir David a twenty-first birthday party last night. A marvelous affair with quite a few eligible young women, but David got so tongue-tied he spent almost no time with them." Sheila lowered her voice. "Mum tells me he's never had a girlfriend. Now don't get me wrong; he likes women well enough, but he's shy beyond belief. He mocks himself by saying he gets along fine with the fairer sex, as long as they're under seven or over seventy!"

Bella thought about what her friend had said. "Oh, I know a few ways to help him overcome his shyness!"

"Bella! Shame on you! What's got into you?!"

"Well, Sheila, my time away at boarding school may have limited my exposure to boys, but Sir David and I clicked at a deep and fundamental level. What to do, what to do?" She shook her head in exasperation. "I'm leaving tomorrow and that won't change." Her stubbornness allowed a brief *Well then, I won't go to America* flit through her mind but her practical nature didn't allow this unthinkable thought to perch there for long.

Sheila looked at her friend with concern. "You look as though someone stepped on your grave?"

Bella made a face. "Och, I'm sad I'll be leaving tomorrow without getting to know Sir David better. But I believe everything happens for a reason. I don't understand why my path crossed with his, but I'm glad it did."

Fiona came back with George to sit with Bella and Sheila, laughing and breathing hard. "I swear your Da played an extra-long tune just to see me huff and puff!"

"It's good for you, Auntie, gets the blood racing!" Sheila grinned. "Do you suppose they'll have Scottish music in California?"

A discussion started of what life in California might be like. Bella had read everything she found in the local library regarding America and proclaimed herself the 'expert' on the history and geography. She knew of the gold rush and the sequoias and the heat and the earthquakes, but little about the practicalities of living there. The foursome became so engrossed in their conversation they didn't notice a shy diffident lad sidle into range. It was George who first felt they were not alone. He looked up and leapt to his feet. "Sir David!"

Three female heads whipped around with various looks of amazement, concern, interest, excitement and hope flitting by. Fiona and Sheila stood and bobbed a curtsy. Bella stayed seated.

David swayed from side to side while hopping from foot to foot, always in danger of falling flat on his face, his discomfort obvious to all. His eyes alternated between a pebble on the road, Bella and Bella's mum. George took a step towards Bella and David, but the gamekeeper, Tam, materialized by David's side. Any further advance by George would have led to trouble between the two ex-soldiers. The sudden tension in the air bypassed David. At last he turned to Fiona and cleared his throat. And cleared his throat again. And again.

"Uh, Mistress, may I ask, ahem, is this your daughter?"

"Yes Sire, this is Bella."

"Right. May I, um, ask your daughter to dance with me?"

Once again, a mixture of emotions flooded the group. Delight on Bella's part; concern from Fiona; George angry; Tam resigned. Sheila thought this the most exciting thing ever to happen in Ballboyne!

Fiona made up her mind; after all, her options were few. One didn't ignore a request from the nobility. Besides, the family were off to America in the morning so what harm would come of it? Fiona had a strong romantic streak herself and this unexpected turn of events pleased her.

"Aye, you can ask!" Fiona sidestepped the responsibility as her tone implied Bella might still say no. She snuck a quick peek at her daughter. *"Fat chance!"* she thought, *"Bella's almost jumping off the wall!"*

David nodded his thanks, turned, looked at the pebble, looked at Bella, looked at the flowers behind her, cleared his throat, looked at Bella again. "Would you like to …? May I have the pleasure…?" David reddened to a ripe raspberry shade, Tam rolled his eyes and Fiona tried not to laugh. George relaxed and stepped back, realizing this embarrassed soul wasn't a threat to his sister. Sheila almost jumped in to help David finish a sentence, any sentence, when Bella hopped off the wall and said, "Yes, I'd love to!" She held out her hand to David who led her off into the crowd of dancers.

Harry Gordon had seen the interplay between Sir David and his family and, as Queen Victoria had once said, was not amused, for the same reasons as George had explained a few minutes past. He caught Dr. Mutch's eye and brought the current dance, a waltz, to a premature end. Before Dr.

Mutch chose the next tune, Harry started a schottische, but a schottische like no one had heard before. A schottische is played in polka time, but Harry sped it up! The dancers looked at each other in surprise, then took on the challenge and hastened to stay with the rhythm. Point, heel, point, heel, step, step, step, step, turn. Point, heel, point, heel, step, step, step, step. Lads, take your lassies in your arms, twirl with her, skirl with her! And do it all again! The crowd got into the spirit of the thing and jumped and juked and yelled and shouted in many of the right places. David and Bella were in the thick of things, laughing and enjoying themselves. Fiona saw two young people having a good time, no class distinctions, no concern about tomorrow, a couple living in the moment, although a noisy moment to be sure. One thing missing was the opportunity for quiet, romantic conversation. Harry's plan had worked!

The tune came to an end and, before David and Bella caught their breaths, Fiona, George, Sheila, even Harry who had abandoned his box, rushed forward to form a protective semi-circle around Bella. Tam sped to David's side, keeping a close eye on Bella's big brother who was whispering in her ear. Bella tossed her head in disagreement, disdain and dismissal. The rest of the dancers caught the group tension and seeped away from the seven protagonists, leaving them like the bulls-eye on a target.

David was still holding Bella's hands, a broad smile on his face, panting like an overheated spaniel. She had her head cocked to the side and her eyes locked onto his. David squeezed her hands. Bella looked down at the unexpected pressure and recoiled in horror. She snatched her hands away from his, turned and fled to the safety of the empty cottage, leaving behind a very bewildered group of people. David started after her but it was Tam, not George, who got in his way.

"No Sire, leave her be! Now is not the time!"

Fiona and Sheila chased after Bella to see what had gone wrong. Harry and George, mere men, did what men do best when confronted with emotional upheaval, they disappeared. Harry returned to his box and started to play again, a slow waltz this time. George pushed open the door to the King's Arms and swigged half of his pint of McEwan's in one gulp.

Chapter 5

Tam steered David to where they had hitched their horses. David was in shock.

"What happened, Tam? Everything seemed to be going well." He stopped short, consternation written all over his face. "Who is she? What's her full name? Do you know anything of her family?"

"I don't, Sire, but I will by tomorrow night. As for what happened, I didn't notice. I kept an eye on the big lad, he didn't seem too fond of you. Can you go over in your mind the sequence of events?" This was an old trick Tam had picked up while soldiering in India and had used before with David.

They had arrived at their horses, but David stopped and closed his eyes. "We had finished the dance and you lot showed up. We were still out of breath and were just standing there. I was holding her hands and gave them a squeeze." David mimed his actions, his hands held out in front of him.

Tam exploded in laughter, David's eyes shot open, annoyed and confused. "What's so bloody funny?"

"Exactly, Sire!" Tam tried to keep a straight face, but failed in suppressing his grin.

"What the hell do you mean?"

"Look at your hands, Sire."

David looked, and everything became clear. His hands were still covered in blood from cleaning the matriarch! In fact, his hands, wrists, elbows and sleeves were plastered in gore.

"Good heavens, she must have thought I'm Jack the Ripper! No wonder she ran!"

"Weel, I'll get word to her tomorrow and clear it up."

"Ah yes, tomorrow." David seemed to grow older for a brief second, a weight settling on his shoulders. Then he shook his head. "Tomorrow will come soon enough. Come on, let's make sure the tenants are getting their fair share of the venison." And young David pointed Haddock towards Castle Cranach.

He turned to speak to Tam again but a gunshot exploded, the bullet spinning David around and throwing him off his horse.

#

Tam jumped from his horse and threw himself over David who was groaning in pain and wheezing for breath. The two ghillies looked on in shock, not understanding what had just happened.

"Hamish, get my gun, load it and pass it over. Angus, catch Haddock. Quick now." The urgency in Tam's voice overcame the ghillies' astonishment and they ran to comply with Tam's orders.

“Thanks, lads. Right, I want you two to ride up to that birch thicket. I think that’s where the shot came from. See what you can find. Carefully now, keep your guns loaded but on safety.” The two ghillies galloped away.

Tam kept looking around for the attacker but couldn’t see him. Nevertheless, he kept his body between Sir David and the probable direction of the assailant. Tam squatted by David. “Let’s see the damage, Sire.” David’s breath was coming back but he still held his chest, groaning. “Here, Sire, let me get your jacket off. Your shirt too. But there’s hardly any blood, how can that be?” Tam bent closer in the fading evening light. “That’s odd. You’ve got a big bruise just below your chest bone but there’s just a wee break in the skin. Clean it with an antiseptic or a splash of good alcohol and you’ll be fine once the bruise heals.”

“Why didn’t the bullet go through me, Tam” David was still wheezing.

“Let me look at your jacket.” Tam picked it up from David’s side to examine. “Huh, it’s as good as new. Well I’ll be damned, look at your spotting scope case. The buckle’s bent and broken.” Tam held the case to his ear and shook it, hearing the broken glass tinkling around inside. “The bullet may still be in there or maybe it ricocheted away. If the bullet hadn’t hit the buckle…” His voice trailed to a stop as he thought the unthinkable.

David could take a deep breath at last. “Tam, did you see who shot at me?”

The two ghillies trotted back, shaking their heads. “No Sire, I believe he’s long gone. We’ll keep a keen eye out for anyone ill-disposed towards you, we have guns after all. Now, Sire, can you get back on your horse?”

Chapter 6

The night inched by. Fiona and Sheila had found Bella in tears, standing over the kitchen sink, washing her hands a la Lady Macbeth. She was hiccupping, gasping and gulping for air, sobbing as though her heart would burst. Fiona took her in her arms. "What's wrong, dear? What upset you? Did Sir David say something?"

"No, Ma! It was his hands!"

"What about his hands?" Fiona's voice rose. "Did he touch you…?"

"No, Ma! His hands were covered in blood!"

"What?" Neither Fiona nor Sheila understood.

"What do you mean, 'covered in blood'?" Sheila's turn.

"Just as I said, he was soaked in blood right up to his elbows, his jacket as well!" Bella dissolved into blubbing again.

"I don't understand! There must be an explanation, don't you think?" Fiona again.

"What possible explanation is there? But even if he has a good reason, why would he ask me to dance when his hands are bloody?" Clearly, David was at fault for everything.

Sheila, ever the romantic, changed the subject. "Does he dance well?"

Bella paused while her mind chose a new path. "Oh, fine, fine! He's light on his feet and a beautiful leader!" The memory of their dance together calmed her for a moment, followed by a fresh wave of agony as she remembered him squeezing her hands. "We were standing there looking at each other and he pressed my hands. I looked down and saw the blood and ran. I just ran!" She broke into tears again.

Fiona and Sheila took turns trying to console Bella, but with little success. The girl had wound herself up as tight as a clock spring. Around ten o'clock, her father and brother tottered in. They'd been enjoying the farewell drinks bought for them by their friends. Harry sobered up some when he saw Bella's state.

"What's the matter, my Bonnie?" he said. This time it was the three women taking turns to interrupt each other, but at last Harry and George understood what had happened, bloody hands and all. George burst into laughter.

"Sis, for a' your learning, you can be a right dimwit! Sir David's no' a mass murderer! He'd come off the hill, he'd been hunting and bagged a prime doe. I hear he worked alongside the ghillies cleaning it. No wonder he's a' bloody!"

Bella stopped her keening while she thought this over. As the truth sank in, first she felt relieved to find her hero on the black horse was innocent of slaughter. But then she felt foolish and embarrassed. "Oh, Ma! Whatever is he to think of me, running away like a wee bairn at the sight of a spot of blood?"

George noticed the amount of blood she had seen had shrunk considerably but kept his mouth shut.

"Bella! You'll not be seeing him again so it doesn't matter!" Fiona became exasperated. "Enough of this nonsense; get over to your Auntie's house with Sheila and off to bed."

Bella opened her mouth to protest but saw her father would support his wife and decided to surrender. The cousins took their leave.

Chapter 7

Now nudging fifty, 'Baron Tookov' bustled through the lobby of New York's Iroquois Hotel as though he owned this grand establishment. John Watkins, his bookkeeper, struggled to keep pace. They ignored the cheery "Good evening, gentlemen!" of the elevator boy, as usual. Also as usual, they didn't tip him. And also as usual, missed the elevator boy mouthing "Miserable cheapskates!" to the closing brass doors. The 'Baron', short and rotund, had a full head of grey hair, swept back at the temples, and long, curled whiskers, the height of fashion at the beginning of the twentieth century. His clothing exuded quality. It should, London's Savile Row tailors had hand-stitched it for him to demonstrate elegance, even here in New York. "All the better to impress the marks!" he would say. He had a cigar in one hand and an ebony topped cane in the other. Despite his lack of physical stature, he had *presence.* Tookov turned to Watkins.

"So, is everything ready for our move to Boston?"

Watkins appeared...average. Or plain. Or nondescript. Unremarkable in every way. Average height, average weight, average coloring, even his clothing, although well-tailored and expensive, seemed to blend him into his surroundings. No one would have picked him out of a police lineup which was fortunate for Watkins because he was as bent as a bobby pin. He wore the mantle of precision as befitted an accountant, as meticulous in his bookkeeping as in his dress, scrupulous in every way…well, except his morals. Proud of and passionate regarding accuracy, he took particular care with his opinions and always hesitated before he committed himself by expressing his thoughts as words.

A floor passed before he said "Yes." Another hesitation. Another floor. "Everything *I'm* responsible for is ready."

Did I detect a hint of reproach? Did Watkins suspect anything? Tookov couldn't be sure. *Maybe Watkins needs more buttering up.*

"Right! Come in and have a drink with me!" Tookov pulled the reluctant bookkeeper out of the elevator, along the corridor and into his luxurious suite.

"You know I don't drink!" Watkins pulled his arm away. "And you know you drink too much!"

Tookov sighed to himself. *This is so tiresome! I can't wait for this teetotal cretin to be out of my life!* But he put on a cheerful face and cozened up to the accountant. "You're right, I drink too much when I'm under strain. Like now. Detectives from the Pinkerton agency have been sniffing around. Do you know who hired them?"

Pause. Thought. "No."

"Lord Adam Rennie of Crachan, the Scottish noble. The one who invested in the mine in Arkansas two years back. He came to his senses at last and hired Pinkerton to investigate us." Tookov took a pull on his chin. "If Rennie stays at

Crachan, we'll be fine. My second son, Michael, is in the Army and I pulled a few strings with my contacts at the War Office to have him transferred to Scotland. Michael'll send me a telegram if he hears of any travels M'Lord is planning. Well, we knew they would catch up to us. Now we must make a new start and where better than Boston, land of the bluebloods. They'll fall for my fiddle like birds out of a tree! Have you ever noticed the more money they have, the greedier they get? They'll be climbing over themselves to get shares in a successful silver mine. Thanks, by the way, for doctoring the assay report."

A pause. "Not at all. My pleasure."

"And you've performed miracles with the annual returns. Our clients are thrilled!"

They both laughed, knowing the reports weren't worth the stamp on the envelope.

"Mr. Watkins, I've been reflecting on our agreement. When we get to Boston, we need to take another look at it. You're not getting your fair share of the profits."

A longer silence this time. "Why, thank you, Baron Tookov, thank you! I always look forward to discussing money."

"Very good, Mr. Watkins. So, I'll see you at the Hotel Vendome in Boston on Tuesday of next week?"

"Yes sir!"

That's better, more spirit, more enthusiasm, misplaced though it may be.

"Good. Good. Until Tuesday, then. Good night!"

#

Tookov closed the door, strode over to the liquor cabinet and poured himself a large whisky. *Drink too much! What a mouse! He'll need a drink when he gets to Boston and discovers I'm nowhere to be found! And I've cleaned out the bank accounts! Good bye, Mr. Watkins! Salut!* He tossed back his whisky. *Now, let's see those bearer bonds and tomorrow's ticket to St. Louis.*

Chapter 8

It took Sir David forever to descend Castle Crachan's stairs for breakfast the next day. He might have attributed his lethargy to a slow recovery from his twenty-first birthday celebrations. He might also have told himself the hunt the previous day had tired him. Then there was the cricket-ball-sized bruise on his chest to consider. Or he might have blamed his lack of sleep on the dreams he had had of the mysterious lassie by the bridge.

Ach, you know why you're dragging your feet. You've got to meet Father and brother James after breakfast. Snap out of it!

Sure enough, when he pushed open the dining room door, there they were, waiting for him. Lord Adam Rennie held court at the head of the long, polished oak table of course, his back to the crackling fire. James sat on his right, as befitted the eldest son and heir, with his recent bride, Agnes, beside him. David's mother, Lady Elspeth, had marooned herself at the opposite end.

The atmosphere was pregnant with tension and ill-will, matching the darkness of the day outside. The fine weather of yesterday had fled during the night, replaced by the wet, windy misery of a Scottish autumn day.

"Glad you made it!" James carped. He was short and thin, cadaverous even at twenty-two years of age. David couldn't help comparing his brother to Uriah Heep, the unctuous character in his favorite book, *David Copperfield.* David ignored his brother, gave his mother a hug, nodded to Agnes and walked to the head of the table.

"My Lord!" he said, bowing over his father's hand.

"David! What's this I hear about you getting yourself shot. That's disgraceful. Tell me all."

"I don't know much, Father, I'd been hunting at Dhoulain Corrie and was on the footpath this side of the Dee Bridge when a shot came from a thicket upstream. The bullet struck the buckle on the case of my spotting scope and winded me. I've got a beautiful black and blue bruise to prove it. If it hadn't hit my buckle, I'd be dead."

The collective intake of breath sounded like the sea emptying from a cave. Even David's mother showed some emotion.

"Did you see who it was?"

"No Sire, none of us did."

"Why would someone want you dead? Do you owe money?'

"No, Father."

"An affair of the heart perhaps, a jealous husband?

David smiled at the absurdity of the question, "No Sire, I've been wracking my brains and can't think of anyone I've wronged in any way."

James broke in. "People don't get shot for no reason. You must have an idea."

"Well, the best I can come up with is the gunshot came from a military rifle, Tam recognized the sound. It's different from a shotgun, as you know. And the only military around here are at the King's Barracks. Tam's there now talking to the commanding officer. But I still don't know of any slight I've given to any of the soldiers."

"Well, this is most unsettling. You've told the police of course?"

"Yes, Sire, Tam is talking to them as well."

"Very well, please keep me informed." Lord Adam drank a mouthful of coffee. "Let me look at you. Other than an almost bullet wound, none the worse for wear, I see. It seems insignificant now but your 21st was a grand party for a grand occasion! How do you feel?"

"Fine, Sire, and thank you for the party, it was a wonderful evening."

"Good, good. I wonder if you can clear something up for me. There's a rumor going around you had Leviathan in your sights yesterday but missed him on purpose. Is this true?"

"Yes, Sire, it is indeed." David dropped into his chair on his father's left.

Uriah scoffed. "No *real* man would have missed. Admit it, you were still drunk and your shakes made you miss!"

David chose not to rise to the bait and ignored his elder brother, infuriating James all the more.

Lady Elspeth, tall, slim, turned out to perfection as always and ever the peacemaker, interceded. "This will be a challenging day so let's keep it civil. Let's enjoy our breakfast." And so, with her head buried in the family sand, she resumed eating her porridge and cream, gossiping with Agnes about the news she had unearthed at David's party. The men were silent, contemplating the next few hours.

Breakfast came to a merciful end and Lord Rennie suggested the men withdraw to the library. The walls, lined with often-read books, seemed to close in on the trio despite the cheery fire in the hearth. Outside, driven by the autumn gale, fallen leaves rushed hither and yon, swirling into haphazard amber, gold and red eddies, settling like snow until the next gust roused them to dance again.

As Lord Rennie and James fussed over choosing cigars, David took the opportunity to examine his father. Now well into his sixties, Father Time had embraced the patriarch much closer over the past few months. The erect regimental stance had disappeared; he seemed more stooped with every passing day. Gone too was the healthy glow which had characterized him for so long. His face had turned ashen and puffy with mottled pink splotches and worry lines etching what looked like a map of the Scottish river system upon it.

David tried to remember the last time he had seen his father out in the country air, but in vain. Most distressing was the total absence of his father's habitual command and vitality. David had expected - no, had counted on - Lord Rennie's usual strength and decisiveness, but his father seemed to have retreated behind a wall of dithering indifference

Even after the cigars were lit to the smokers' satisfaction, David's father still wouldn't meet his eye. This too was out of character. Meanwhile, James all but hopped from foot to foot in his excitement.

David decided to start the conversation. "My Lord, we all know why we are here. I am your second son. I am now twenty-one and you need my decision as to my future. As is customary, when you pass on, your first son, James," (He nodded in his brother's direction.) "will inherit everything: your title, your lands, your estate. I hope that day will be slow in coming. I need not and do not expect to inherit much more than my title. I must make my own way in the world."

James broke in, "Yes, and the sooner the better. I don't need you sponging off me for years to come…"

Lord Rennie broke in with rare forcefulness. "Enough! Keep a civil tongue in your head! This is difficult enough without us descending into petty bickering!" He looked from son to son. "David, you are right, we need to discuss your future, but there are other important issues to discuss too." James and David glanced at each other, puzzled.

Lord Rennie slumped behind his desk. "First, let's talk of your future, David. You're not the only second son to be eased out of the nest due to birth order. And the precedents would suggest you look at either the ministry or the military." A brief smile caught the corner of Lord Rennie's mouth. "Reverend Sir David Rennie has a certain ring to it, don't you agree?"

David couldn't help himself and laughed. "Thank you, my Lord, but before I taught the Bible, I'd need a firm acquaintance with it and that I am lacking! No, Father, religion is not the road for me."

"I'm relieved, David. I can't see you confined to a parish; you're too vital."

James harrumphed, unable to tolerate his younger brother getting any attention.

Lord Rennie continued: "So we come to the military. You're well aware of how fulfilled I felt by my service in the Scots Guards, and your man Tam no doubt has painted his own picture. I'm sure I can get you a commission in my old regiment if you were so inclined."

David paused. He didn't want to tell his father Tam had indeed "painted his own picture" of military life, and a very negative picture it was. Ineptitude from the War Office down, the lack of clear military objectives, the bigotry, inbreeding and idiocy of the officer corps, the brutality of the NCOs, the appalling living conditions for officers and men, Tam had spared no one in his scathing criticism. David had no desire to be a part of that but he also had no wish to hurt his father's feelings.

"Father, I believe I need to travel more before I choose which life I wish to lead and where I wish to lead it. I've explored Europe; now I wish to go to America …"

Before David could finish, James jumped in. "Well, don't suppose I'm financing your swanning around Texas pretending to be a cowboy!"

Lord Rennie lurched to his feet and rounded on James. "You may be my heir, but do *not* presume to speak on my behalf!" David enjoyed hearing the spirit in his father's voice and didn't much mind James being put in his place.

Lord Rennie paused, lost in thought, then continued. "Your attraction to America pleases me, David. You may be able to help me a great deal. I need both of you to listen with care." Another pause, and this time he seemed to steel himself, as though he were about drink a glass of poison. "If the estate's finances do not improve, I will be bankrupt by this time next year."

#

Silence. Shock. Disbelief.

James erupted. "What the hell do you mean, 'bankrupt'? How could you be bankrupt? What of my inheritance? What will I tell Agnes?" He was shouting now, his pale face darkening with wrath.

"Keep a civil tongue in your head and do *not* forget to whom you are speaking!" The steel came back to Lord Rennie's voice. He stood taller, commanding and competent, in charge again. "Your 'inheritance' is still mine to leave to whomsoever I wish. One more self-absorbed outburst and I will change my will."

More disbelief from James. His father had never spoken to him in such a manner. The older brother spluttered, but held his tongue. There was no doubt Lord Rennie meant what he said. James slouched into an armchair by the fire.

David intervened. "You said my traveling to America might be to your advantage. What do you have in mind, My Lord, and when would this happen?"

Lord Rennie smiled at his younger son. "Always so eager! The 'when' is easy: as soon as practical. The 'what' will take explaining, including how I got into this mess."

More hesitation from the Lord as he sank behind his desk again, then began a long, sad, confession. "It started ten years ago with a 'chance' meeting with a supposed Russian called Baron Pyotr Tookov at my club in London. Your uncle Lord Milne introduced him and Tookov showed me a sheaf of introductions from all over Europe, so I trusted him." Lord Rennie sighed. "Exiled from the Russian court, Tookov said he had been making the rounds of the European royals and soon would return to America where he had made successful investments in gold and silver mines. The British economy had been in a slump for many years so I was interested in investing elsewhere and asked for more information. He showed me a prospectus for a silver mine in Arkansas."

"Where's Arkansas, my lord?"

"Somewhere near the middle of America, quite underdeveloped I understand." Lord Rennie waved his hand.

"Anyway, I had my solicitor and accountant look at the figures and they both liked what they saw, so much so they sank much of their own life savings into it."

James stared at the fire, looking as though he was about to be a major participant in a train wreck. David listened, noted, analyzed, filing away names and dates and places.

"How much have we invested, Sire?"

Lord Rennie looked stricken. "Everything. Twice a year Tookov would send certified statements showing how well the mine had performed, the amount of silver being taken out, the impressive size of the mother lode. He suggested I re-invest the profits so I would become the majority shareholder. In retrospect, I realize those suggestions always came as soon as he had sent the latest round of good news. At first, he would send me bank drafts too, returns on my investments, he called it. And handsome returns they were, but they ceased two years past. The statements also stopped coming and I made enquiries. That's when I found out I had been duped. I and many others."

Lord Rennie's forcefulness had deserted him and indecisiveness threatened to take over again.

James, ever one to exploit a weakness, turned on him. "You are a fool, Father, an old, incompetent, utter fool! How could you do this to me?" He stood up, his hands balled, looking for a chance to strike the older man, but David stepped in between them. For a moment, the two brothers faced each other, toe-to-toe, eyeball to eyeball. At last James came to his senses and backed off, realizing his twenty-pound weight disadvantage would not help him in a brawl with his well-seasoned younger brother.

David turned to his father again. Never one to waste time in regret, he asked what his father wanted him to do.

"Well, there is a mine. It's called the Evening Star and it lies somewhere near Rush in Arkansas. I understand there's been no activity at the mine for almost five years, but it has some color. I know it's grasping at straws but I want you to go to Arkansas and look at it. Find out whether it has any value and report back. You must go to Glasgow first to talk to my lawyer and accountant. They're in shock too, but want to help in any way they can."

David nodded, his father continued.

"I hired a detective agency in New York. I want you to see them when you land there. They worked in concert with the London Metropolitan Police and issued a joint report." Lord Rennie took a deep breath and his sons saw the tension leave him as he exhaled. He had faced his demon and the telling of it had purged his soul. "How soon can you leave, David? And will your bruised chest hinder you at all?"

James jumped in again, a little less shrill this time. "My Lord, I am the elder son; I should be the one to go!"

Lord Rennie shook his head. "James, this is not the time to stand on formalities such as who is my firstborn son and heir. We need the best person doing the job he's best at. I need you here by my side to run the estate, both now and in the future. That's what you're best at doing. I need David prowling around America finding everything he can about this mine. That's the kind of project he does best. We need to work together to get out of this mess."

David admired the adroit way his father had handled his first son. *James running around in America? A preposterous thought. He'd have lost himself in London's Hyde Park!* David glanced at James and saw his brother sigh in relief.

"The bruise won't delay me, I can leave within the week, my Lord. May I take Tam with me?"

Lord Rennie hesitated for a moment while he fought with his jealousy of Tam's influence on his son. Good sense prevailed as the benefits were clear. "Yes, of course, he'll be indispensable to you."

Lord Rennie turned to the table behind his desk and picked up a box stuffed with papers. "Read these, David. They're all the information I have regarding this wretched affair. I hope you can make sense of them."

Chapter 9

David and James left the Library together, leaving Lord Rennie staring out the window. David had the eerie feeling his father had shrunk again. As soon as they closed the door, James rounded on him.

"How could he do this to me? Bankrupt! We'll be the laughing stock of the county, no, of Scotland! And what do I tell Agnes? She's already after me to make this place more comfortable, with no thought to cost!"

James kept cackling on like a demented hen, but made no mention of their father or had any suggestions of how to get out of this mess. David let James drone on while his mind raced with unconnected thoughts: *How do I get to America, what shall I ask the detectives, how much should I tell Tam, should I take my rifle, what's the name of the lassie on Bridge Street? Hello? Where did she come from?*

James must have sensed he had an audience of none. "David, I'm talking to you! You must help me. What do I say to Agnes? How much do I tell her?"

David almost smiled. He didn't have a high opinion of Agnes on a good day, which this wasn't. She was too quick to gossip about others, making David wary of what she might say of his family. David wasn't surprised to hear she had no close friends, gossips aren't trusted and so live a solitary life of their own making. Agnes and James' wedding was less than a year ago but already it was clear who wore the breeches.

"You must tell her the truth, of course. But you don't have to tell her anything she doesn't ask. For instance, if she asks you why we met this morning, tell her we were looking at a plan for the estate's finances. You don't have to tell her about the mining investment or the potential for bankruptcy."

"Potential? You imagine there's hope then?"

David sighed. James was looking for a miracle cure, but David didn't have the heart to douse him with a bucket of cold, sobering reality. "I'll know more when I've gone through this," he said, motioning with the box of papers. "Now, please excuse me, I want to get started. Tam!" he shouted, "Where are you?" Tam materialized at his side. "Take this box. Come with me." David strode off to his suite in the East Wing, focused, intent, with Tam in hot pursuit.

James dithered, unwilling to face Agnes, yet in need of someone to talk to. His abhorrence of being alone won and he went in search of his bride.

#

"Get our horses ready, Tam."

Tam blinked at David's command. This was not what he had expected. Tam looked out the window at the hard, cold rain angling sideways on the wind. His military training kicked in, "Yes, Sire." David's tone of voice brooked no questions. "And the box?"

"Lock it in my bureau and keep the key with you at all times. No one— and I mean no one—is to see inside the box except at my say-so and in my presence. Right, horses in five minutes, please."

Tam passed David's request on to the grooms, secured the box and hurried off to get oilskins to keep them as dry as possible. All the while, he was trying to make sense of what had happened.

Tam and the rest of the staff knew David's twenty-first birthday would cause significant change and was the purpose of this morning's meeting. *But why the box? What was so valuable it required such handling? Why was David so ... masterful?* On the other hand, Tam hadn't expected James to be so indecisive. *He must have had his status as first son and heir affirmed; why wasn't he elated instead of trembling like a birch leaf in a breeze.* Mary, Lady Agnes' maid and Tam's latest paramour, would tell him all. *And why on earth were they going riding in this foul weather?*

David and Tam set off, willing their reluctant mounts into the wind and rain. Tam had brought scarves to seal their necks from the cold trickle threatening to circumvent their oilskins. They rode side by side up the bridle path through the pine forest behind the Castle. David was silent and intense, Tam refrained from interrupting, knowing David would talk when ready. They had ridden for half an hour when David pulled his horse to a stop under a rocky overhang which afforded a slight protection from the weather. "Tam, the family is in trouble and I need to fix it."

"Yes, Sire." What else could Tam say?

“I’m off to America. I’ll be in New York before going to Arkansas to look for a silver mine.”

“I see, Sire. When do we leave?”

David almost cracked a smile. “Thank you, Tam, your loyalty humbles me. But I want you to give considerable thought before you agree to come with me. I’ll be gone for months. I don’t know what I’ll be up against. I don’t know the size of the problem so I don’t have any solutions. I don’t even know if I want to come back to Ballboyne.” Unbidden, a flash of the Bridge Street lassie’s smile chased over his eyes. He shook his head to clear it.

Back to Ballboyne? For a moment, Tam wondered why David had mentioned the village rather than the estate. Then he remembered the stunning beauty of last evening and knew the answer.

Tam interrupted David’s pause. “We’d better get started then. Do you have a plan? And where the hell is Arkansas?”

David sighed with relief. He couldn’t have made Tam come with him if Tam hadn’t wanted to.

“I want to leave as soon as possible. There’s considerable urgency to this matter. As for Arkansas, it’s in the middle of America and not well-developed, that’s all I know. This is what we need to do …” and so started a long, detailed discussion of what had to be accomplished in the next few days: passports, letters of credit, clothing, guns …the list grew and grew. Tam would record everything once he returned to the Castle and would have plenty of questions in the ensuing days but at least now he knew why he was sitting on a horse in a downpour. David needed space to think.

#

With Tam busy organizing the packing, David found shelter in his study and settled in with a fine Glendullan single malt to digest the box of papers detailing Lord Rennie's 'investment'. David soon found his fears confirmed. The high initial returns had charmed Lord Rennie into giving up close inspection of the information Tookov had sent and had accepted it at face value.

By the end of the afternoon, David had deduced there was indeed a mine called the Evening Star near the town of Rush in Marion County, Arkansas. The mine had shown color at one time, as proved by a report from a certified government assay agent; eight percent silver, it had said. Lord Rennie owned the majority of the shares, 90 percent, with the remaining shares split between his accountant and his solicitor.

The combined report from the London Metropolitan Police and the American detective agency, Pinkerton, made particularly depressing reading. David learned how Baron Tookov was Peter Thomas, a London con artist who had fled to America after bilking British investors of hundreds of thousands of pounds and how he was just as successful in New York but had disappeared with the police threatening to arrest him. His current whereabouts were unknown, although Pinkerton thought there was slim possibility that he had gone to tie up loose ends in Arkansas.

David sighed. The future of the family's fortune was indeed in serious doubt.

Next day, David met with his father and James to explain his intentions and to detail what help he needed from the Estate. Lord Rennie delighted at David's decisive grasp of the fiasco and agreed to take charge of the necessary telegrams. These would introduce David to Lord Rennie's lawyer and accountant in Glasgow, and to the head of the Pinkerton agency and the British Consul General, one Sir Jonathan Smythe, both in New York. Lord Rennie would also write Letters of Introduction for David to present. The older man was a traditionalist and didn't trust these new-fangled telegraphs.

David put Lord Rennie's mind at ease regarding the delicate topic of who would pay the expenses for this excursion to America.

"My Lord," he said, "I plan on paying my expenses out of the inheritance your uncle left me. Perhaps we can look on it as a loan, repayable if I am successful and not if I am unsuccessful. It will double my incentive to bring this Tookov to justice!"

Lord Rennie had protested, a little, but agreed. James had jumped at the idea, then went in search of his owner, Agnes.

Before David left, Lord Rennie asked him to stay a moment to look at a map. However, once James had closed the door behind him, Lord Rennie confessed he had wanted to speak to David alone.

“This isn’t for James’ ears, David. He’s not mature enough to see the benefit in what I plan for you.”

David didn’t understand.

“Give me a guinea, please!”

David’s confusion grew, but he did as asked, pulling the coin from his pocket.

“Thank you. You are now the majority owner of the Evening Star mine! When you see my solicitor in Glasgow, he’ll require you to sign the papers to make it official.”

“I don’t follow, Father?”

“I don’t know if there is any value to the mine, and I wouldn’t expect it to be in operation. It seems the best way to recoup anything would be to sell it. If you’re the owner, you’ll be able to make quick decisions without having to wait for instructions telegraphed from Scotland.” A smile twitched his lips. “I’ll still expect you to compensate me in full if you manage to pull money out of this mess!”

“Of course, Father, of course! And thank you!” David saw the sense in his father’s actions; maybe the old boy wasn’t quite ready for the knacker’s yard! He left in search of Tam to assign him more tasks. For a moment, he wondered if his friend could handle the load, but dismissed the idea, laughing. Tam’s military experience had taught him how to delegate and he would have the whole castle staff helping him by now!

Chapter 10

Bella and family tossed and turned in their borrowed accommodations at Harry's sister Kate's cottage. It was a tight squeeze for the four of them, but it seemed as though their adventure had begun: new experiences, new sounds, even the beds felt foreign. Bella managed to find a deep sleep as dawn snuck in over the windowsill. Fiona had trouble waking her but Bella's reluctance at re-entering the world of the living vanished when she remembered what the day promised.

"Come on, lazybones, we've a big day ahead of us!"

"All right, Ma, I'm awake!"

"How are you this morning?"

"Tired, I didn't sleep until the cock crowed. How could I have been so foolish?"

"You're talking of Sir David, aren't you? Did you come to any conclusions?"

"Yes, Ma. Last night I longed to see him again. Now I hope he never sets eyes on me. I'd die of embarrassment."

Fiona nodded in understanding. "Maybe it's a good idea we're leaving today so you won't have to face him. Chalk it up to experience, my dear." As Bella nodded, Fiona shifted focus, "All right, up with you. Better dress for weather, Mrs.

McPhee's forecast was accurate, I'm sad to say. It's a wild day outside."

As Bella washed up and slipped into her clothes, she heard the storm battering against the cottage and saw the treetops whipping back and forth like a two-handed saw worked by invisible giants. The doors and windows leaked drafts at the best of times, but this gale had the curtains standing away from the walls and the rooms stayed chilled despite the cheery coal fire along the hallway in the kitchen. Freak gusts sent the smoke billowing back down the chimney and filled the wee cottage with a thick, smothering fug.

"Good morning, Auntie Kate, where is everybody?"

Kate turned from the hearth. She was a good-natured woman with a ready smile and a big heart. "Oh, they're up and away, sleepyhead! George ran up to the station to borrow old Jock's luggage cart. He'll meet up with your Da at your old house and they'll load the cart with your trunks and valises and take them up to the station. George will have your belongings locked in the luggage room."

"Where's Ma? I haven't seen her since she woke me."

"She's gone to your house with Sheila, finishing up the cleaning, though what there's left to scrub I wouldn't know. It's already spotless."

Bella laughed. "Isn't that a fact? She's been scouring non-stop for a month now. The folks moving in will have nothing to clean, just bring in their furniture." She paused. "And how's Uncle Andrew this morning?" She had best broach this touchy subject with care.

Kate tamped down an angry reply. “He’s sleeping it off, as usual.” A cloud slipped by her eyes. “He enjoyed last night’s party as much as anyone, also as usual. He’ll never change; he’s a drunk, which means we’ll never follow you to America. I’ll miss my favorite niece!”

Bella laughed at the old joke. “May I remind you I’m still your only niece?” Then Bella turned serious again. “I’m sorry about Uncle Andrew, Auntie Kate. He’s good man when he’s sober.”

“Yes, he is, and, I’m happy to say, he’s a sociable drunk when he’s not. I never worry about him hitting me, he hasn’t a mean bone in his body. He gets romantic too, so there are side benefits!” Kate laughed and Bella blushed.

“What does Da want me to do?” She asked, making an obvious change of topic.

Kate laughed again. “We never did have a talk about boys and romance, did we? Ah well, too late now. Let me say you’ll know when you meet the right man, but keep your guard up until then.”

It was on the tip of Bella’s tongue to tell Kate about Sir David but Harry’s return from the station interrupted them.

“Well, the baggage’s taken care of.” He rubbed his hands in front of the fire. “Man, we’ve got a snell wind out there. You wouldn’t have a nice hot cup of tea for your auld brother, would ye now, Kate?”

"I can get you more than a cuppa, Harry, here's your breakfast. You were away too early for me to get it ready for you before. You too, Bella, sit and eat."

Harry drew a chair out from the table. "Oh my! Bacon and egg and sausage and fried bread! You've outdone yourself, lassie!"

Kate colored. "Och, away with you. There's toast and my marmalade too!" She poured the black, steaming tea into the china cups, her best china cups.

Bella noticed this honor and somehow it brought into focus the enormity of the day. It wasn't only the journey ahead of them, weeks on trains and boats, but the leaving behind everyone and everything she cherished. The canvas she saw looking backwards was full and understandable, but when she looked ahead, the canvas was blank, the horizon empty. For the first time since she'd been told the family was emigrating, she felt afraid.

Kate, observant as ever, saw Bella blanch. "What's the matter, dearie?"

Bella tried to laugh it off, then, after coaxing and prodding by her elders, surrendered and told her aunt and her Da what had upset her. "It was the blank canvas. I can't see what my life will be in America!" To her surprise, her Da answered her, not Kate.

"It is a blank canvas, isn't it? I must admit I've seen a blank canvas more times than I'd care to say. I found it worst in the wee small hours of the morning and I lost a lot of sleep over it. At last, for my own sanity, I decided I would look at the canvas in a different way, not as the great unknown where nasty beasties lurk, but as the canvas I can paint my own picture on." He took a swig of tea. "I see our canvasses fitting together but being different too. Mine will have big broad strokes, while your Ma's will be more detailed, more precise, a flower garden maybe. George's will be big and bold too. What will yours look like?"

Bella laughed, "I have no idea, but it will differ from here. Thanks, Da, you've helped me a lot. A canvas I can design for myself. Yes!"

Harry said, "I have one last thing to do. Come with me, please, Bella!" They walked the few yards back to their old home, hunching into the wind. The cottage was spic and span, yet empty and forlorn. Fiona and George joined them as Harry picked up the old whisky case from the front step and carried it to the peak of the bridge. "Time for me to liberate you too, old man. God speed!" He tossed the box over the parapet into the River Dee and they watched it swirl and eddy and dip and bob and weave, floating in the middle of the fast-flowing river. The current swept it round the curve by the Logieben Estate and the box disappeared.

Chapter 11

It was time: 8:45 in the morning, time for the Gordons to leave, the closing goodbyes said, the last tears wept, the final hugs embraced. It was time to look forward to the trip ahead of them.

George took charge now. He was the world traveler with army experience on three continents. Harry and Fiona taken the train to Aberdeen twice, once on their honeymoon and once for a funeral, so they had limited knowledge of the basic rules of travel. Even Bella had journeyed more often when she went to Aberdeen for school. George and Harry had seen the family's possessions secured in the baggage car and were now ready to help the women climb up into a third-class compartment. George turned the big brass handle to open the door and lowered the door's window using the wide leather strap. First, he lifted Bella onto the wooden step then helped her up into the carriage. Bella turned and took her Mas hand and, with Harry pushing and Bella pulling, Fiona catapulted in to join her.

"Thanks, Harry, you too Bella, I'd never have made it by myself in this long skirt!"

The carriage was empty except for two farmers' wives, short and plump, each with a headscarf tied under one of their chins. The women were taking produce to Aberdeen to sell on The Green. At least one chicken squawked from the luggage rack and a wifie's bag at her feet quacked quietly.

"Here, Ma! Let me put the valises up onto the rack; it'll give us more room."

"Right you are, George. But don't put this bag up anywhere, it's got baps and rowies to eat on the way. Aunt Kate made them this morning, bless her. I miss her already." All of a sudden, Fiona looked close to tears. Bella, sitting next to her, grasped her hand and held it tight.

"Ma, it'll be fine! Remember last night when I got frightened and Da talked about us having a blank canvas to write our future on? Reflect on your canvas when you get afeared. We're off on a great adventure!"

"You're right, Bella." Fiona smiled at the thought of her baby girl giving her advice. "We'll be fine."

Harry sat on the other side of his wife and gave her other hand a squeeze. "We'll be more than fine!" He smiled. "We'll be grrrrand!" The exaggerated accent made them laugh and lifted their spirits.

The engine gathered itself to pull the two carriages the 40 miles from Ballboyne station into Aberdeen, huffing and puffing, smoke from the engine blown sideways by the violent wind. There was a grim beauty to the countryside, despite the weather. The hills gave way to the Dee valley, purple heather to green fields with black Aberdeen Angus cows grazing with supreme indifference to the slanting rain. Here and there a farmer had been too late to cut his wheat and his fields stooped with the ripe but now useless grain. Barley seemed made of stronger stuff and islands of it bobbed and bent and curtsied on the wind while, inches away, similar stalks had collapsed and lay strewn in disarray.

The trip into Aberdeen was long enough for them to get uncomfortable on the wooden benches. But Bella's sleepless night took its toll and soon the rhythmic rocking of the carriage and the hypnotic song of the wheels on the tracks lulled her to sleep, her head resting on her mother's shoulder. "Clickety clack, clickety clack, clickety clack, Banchory, clickety clack, Kincardine O'Neil, clickety clack, Culter, clickety clack." It seemed almost no time before Bella awakened to the stationmaster's singsong voice crying "Aiberdeen! All change, Aiberdeen!"

The Gordon family roused itself and stretched and rubbed their bums. George hustled off to see to the heavy baggage while Harry, Fiona and Bella took care of the valises. George returned with their baggage piled high on a cart propelled by a porter stumping along on a wooden leg. An old soldier by the look of him; he still wore his khaki military jacket with faded sergeant's chevrons on the sleeves. His pants didn't match the jacket and his military boots, while bright as a mirror, appeared to have more hole than sole. His hair, though long, looked clean but it had been many a morning since his chin had graced a razor. The soldier had fallen on hard times, but he still held himself with dignity and pride.

Harry looked at George in exasperation. A porter meant a tip and more money spent. George understood Harry's glare, nodded to the porter, then ran his finger over his own chest. Harry squinted at the porter, noticing for the first time the long row of faded military ribbons. His eyes widened in amazement; the campaign ribbons showed the porter had served all over the British Empire. But the first ribbon stopped Harry cold. A simple ribbon, a faded crimson. Those conversant in such matters—which included Harry—would see the wearer had been awarded the Victoria Cross, Britain's highest military honor "For Valor in the Face of the Enemy." Harry understood, George had wanted to support the old soldier, and a three-penny tip wouldn't hurt the family in the long run. The porter led them to the platform where the Glasgow train departed and the three men loaded the baggage once more into the luggage van. George gave the sergeant his tip and received a nod of the head in acknowledgement.

"Sergeant!" called George.

The soldier turned in surprise.

George drew himself up to his full height, stood at attention, and snapped off a salute that would have made any Regimental Sergeant Major proud. The sergeant's eyes gleamed in appreciation. He stood tall and returned the salute, then turned away to attend to his business. Harry, though he'd missed military service, nodded his approval.

The North British Line train bound for Glasgow still had just the one first class carriage with six compartments, each compartment boasting three padded seats a side with armrests and doilies on the headrests to prevent greasy hair from staining the grey-blue upholstery. The four third class cars which the Gordons sought were similar to the one in which they'd traveled from Ballboyne. Hard wooden seats and seat backs, no concessions made for comfort here.

"What's that awful stink, George?" Bella held her hankie over her nose as they walked towards their carriage. They were passing two covered freight cars, appendages to their train, old and smelling to high heaven.

"Och, that's the fish, Bella. Fish merchants buy them at the market over the road there, their fishwifies clean them, pack them in these long boxes and porters haul them over to these freight cars. Look!" George nodded to a porter crossing the street from the fish market, balancing a large box of fish on a leather cap on his head. "The fish end up in Edinburgh, Glasgow, even London. The railways use the freight cars day in and day out, with a rare acquaintance with a hose. No wonder they reek so much! But it's not all bad, we may not enjoy the stink but *they* love it!" He pointed to a batch of herring gulls walking with impunity through the station and pecking at anything nautical and edible.

Bella soaked up everything she saw and heard. A few minutes before departure, a railwayman walked by with his hammer, tapping every wheel.

"Who's he, George, and what's he doing?"

George smiled with patience and fondness at his little sister. "He's the driver, Bella. Before each trip, he checks every wheel on the train to make sure it's not falling apart."

"But how can he tell with a hammer?"

"He listens to the sound the hammer makes on each wheel. A cracked wheel makes a different sound than a whole one."

"Oh, like a bell!"

"Yes, like you, my cracked little sister!"

Before Bella could punch him on the arm, Harry announced, “Here’s our carriage!” Harry and George once again helped the women into their compartment, hampered as they were by the height of the step and their long woolen skirts. Right on time, the train lurched off on the four-hour journey to Glasgow.

At last, a few minutes past six on a fair west coast evening, the train eased to a halt in Glasgow’s Queen Street Station. George hired a porter with a cart and handled the unloading of the baggage, all the while fending off the touts and tipsters offering best choices in anything one needed, from accommodation to food, from licit to illicit. Back in Ballboyne, fellow soldiers had given George the address of a rooming house, but when he gave this to the porter, the man drew back in disgust.

“Mister, have you ever been to this place?” George had a tough time understanding the hard, thick Glasgow accent, worsened by a whistle, the result of missing teeth. One of those folks of an indeterminate age, he was short and wiry with strong rough hands. Huge ears framed a long, weather beaten, creased face and kept his brown tweed cap up and out of his eyes.

“No.” said George, “Why do you ask?”

“Well, the address you gave me is in the Gorbals, the armpit of Europe, you know! It’s also the toughest place in Europe. You’d be fine, seeing the size of you, but I’d not take the women there in a million years.” He paused and thought over what he had said. “You’ll be thinking I’m trying to drum up business for myself?”

George nodded, “Yes, the thought had occurred, no offense, mind.”

“None taken. Let me put it this way, I won’t take you, it’s more than my life’s worth. You’ll need to find another porter if you’re set on going there. But choose any other place outside the Gorbals and I’m your man. And if you like, I can recommend two or three clean, decent and safe houses. You’re away to America, aren’t you?”

“Aye, how did you know?”

The porter smiled, showing all four of his choppers. “A family traveling with this much baggage isn’t going on holiday! You’ll be sailing from the Port of Glasgow?”

“Yes, in three days’ time, if all goes well.”

“Oh, you mean the medical inspection. Don’t worry; it’s a bit of a formality. So somewhere central would be best.” He rattled off three addresses with descriptions of each one. “They’re within walking distance and they’re clean and cheap.”

Harry had been eavesdropping on the two and interrupted. “What’s your name, sir?”

“Billy, sir, Billy MacBride.”

“George, we mustn’t put the lassies at risk. We should consider Billy’s recommendations.”

“I agree with you, Da.” George turned to the porter and enquired, “If it was you and your family, which one would you choose?”

Billy didn't even hesitate. "Mrs. Duncan, sir, she's a widow, lost her husband over in South Africa. Works hard, cleans well and cooks even better. She doesn't have much space but I'm sure you're used to roughing it yerself."

A little flattery never hurt! thought George. "All right! Gordons, we're following Billy here!" And off they set for the mile and a half walk to Mrs. Duncan's rooming house, Billy trundling the cart with the baggage.

Mrs. Duncan lived in a row house with two stories, a wee front yard and peeling paint on the windows. George regretted his choice at first but then saw the front door sparkled in a new coat of blue paint with burgundy trim, the yard also was spotless and well-tended. The closer he looked, it became clear nothing but a lack of money was holding Mrs. Duncan back. She'd taken care of everything that 'only' required hard work.

George and Billy negotiated with the landlady who welcomed their open purse with open arms. Soon, they had the cabin trunks locked in the cupboard under the stairs and the personal valises carried up to the one room that was to be the Gordon's for the next two nights. Mrs. Duncan rustled up a cup of tea and a bite to eat, then they climbed up to their bedroom. Billy's prediction about roughing it turned out to be prophetic. Their room boasted one bed which Ma and Bella claimed. The men slept on the floor, not much of a hardship for the soldier but Da had a tougher time. The long, long day came to a satisfactory end, but the medical inspection was tomorrow.

Chapter 12

Even Macbeth's witches would have stayed home on the day David and Tam departed Castle Crachan. The unseasonable wintry weather had stayed all week as though mourning the loss of the Castle's last sparks of light and energy. Gales, rain, more rain, more gales had left the countryside beaten, battered and bruised with trees down, the rivers and burns in full spate and many roads and fields flooded. The wicked weather and Tam's nagging made it easier for David to stay within the castle walls, out of gunshot range. His bruise was easing and he no longer winced with each movement.

Dawn was struggling to show itself, even at eight in the morning. Tam told the staff to load their steamer trunks and valises onto the coach and four. The foul weather required David to say his farewells to his family in the great entrance hall of the castle. The goodbyes were strained and unemotional, a brief hug from his mother, an even briefer handshake from his father with the insipid exhortation for David to "do his best," hardly a ringing endorsement of faith and high expectations.

James was his usual feckless self. David's suggestions on how to deal with Lady Agnes had fallen on deaf ears. James' wife now knew of the family's financial shortcomings and had made it clear to James (and everyone else within 100 yards) she wouldn't stand for it and demanded James do something or else…! Her "or else" terrified James and he became a whirlwind of ineptitude, issuing demands and counter-demands and orders and contradictory orders. The staff paid him no heed.

James begged, demanded, pleaded and prayed for David "*to have a successful expedition*", as though David was leaving to search for the source of the Nile. In a rare moment of insight, James had even added, "*I hope we meet again*", a sobering reminder to David this was no pleasure jaunt he was embarking upon.

On the lighter side, David smiled at Tam, yes, Tam's, embarrassment Tam's departure had most of the female staff lined up to say farewell and this caused much weeping and wailing. *My, my, Tam, haven't you been a busy lad!*

The coach set off along the mile-long driveway towards the railway station in Ballboyne. David had always loved this drive, the copper beech tree canopy towering above the muddy track. Last week, they had been in full autumn color but now the winds had stripped them to their bare essentials. On either side of the trees was parkland, punctuated by stands of rhododendrons and azaleas, glorious crimson and mauve when in flower but now a deep, dreary, wet green. Sheep and lambs often dotted the parkland, but today it looked devoid of life, empty, windswept and grim. The coach came to the formal entrance to the estate, imposing rough granite columns with a beam topping them engraved with "Bydandfecht", or "Stand and Fight" in the Scottish vernacular.

"Perfect," thought David. *"Just how I feel."* He allowed the anger he felt towards Baron Tookov boil inside

him for a moment, then set it aside again as being an emotion he could not yet afford.

The coach swung round onto the road leading to Ballboyne. David had one last glimpse of Castle Crachan. *Was he saying goodbye forever to the Castle?* Here stood the Protestant Kirk in the middle of the village with the tall spire soaring high above the square. *Would he ever see these places again?* Then they came to the wee row of shops nestled between the Kirk and the Dee Bridge.

Ah yes, the Dee Bridge and Bridge Street. David called for the coach to slow as he craned his neck, hoping to glimpse the mysterious lassie. Tam, sitting opposite David, had been motionless and silent, but when he saw David's continuing interest in her, he cleared his throat and said "Her name is Bella Gordon, daughter of Harry and Fiona Gordon. She's seventeen and the big lad is her elder brother, George. She's been away in Aberdeen at school and planned on being a tutor, but her father became unemployed when the distillery closed a while back and they decided to join his brother in America. They left two days ago."

David sat back and eyed Tam. He wanted to deny any interest, but he realized it must have been obvious he was love-struck. He felt a surge of deep and bitter disappointment at her sudden departure, but a ray of irrational hope followed. *Might I find her once I get to America?*

"Where in America is the brother, Tam?"

"California, Sir David."

David paused. *Arkansas's in the middle of the country and California's hundreds of miles to the west. Damn!*

"Tam, how did you find out about the Gordons?"

"I asked my … contacts."

I'll bet you did! thought David. *And I'll bet your contacts wore skirts!*

The Ballboyne Railway Station had been built for Queen Victoria's benefit 35 years before. It seemed the few travelers who had ventured out in this wicked weather were those with no choice, those associated with the Royal Household at Balmoral Castle for example. David spied Mrs. Beattie, the Chief Cook, checking in special supplies, one of her scullery maids helping her. Three soldiers from the Castle's guard were there, huddled over the coal fire in the Waiting Room. Unbeknownst to David and Tam, another soldier took an intense interest in them from behind a pillar. The train blew a warning whistle, so Tam found Jock, the ancient porter, who grudgingly agreed to help Tam load the valises into the empty First Class compartment and the cabin trunks into the baggage car. David bought the tickets to Glasgow. They didn't notice the inquisitive soldier leap aboard at the last minute.

The train chuntered away, one final blast on the whistle to remind Ballboyne it was losing two of its finest. "Tam, now we're underway, here's what we'll do. First, I want to travel as incognito as possible. I want to conceal my connection to Lord Rennie, so no more Sir David or Sire. You need to call me Mr. Rennie, or even David. In case there's any danger in store for us, I see no point in advertising who we are. Do you understand?"

"Yes, Sire … I mean, David … I mean Mr. Rennie. Och, this will be hard, but I'll be comfortable in addressing you as Mr. Rennie before we get to America."

"Good man. When we get to Glasgow this afternoon, I'll be seeing Lord Rennie's accountant and solicitor. While I'm meeting with them, I want you to get our baggage aboard the SS Curambria, it's lying offshore in the Port of Glasgow. I'll join you there later. We sail at eight this evening. I've got a first-class cabin; you'll be in second-class. I want you to pump the passengers and crew as much as possible concerning Tookov. It would be a huge coincidence if he were ever close to the Curambria, but one never knows. See if you can find anything out regarding Arkansas too. Also, my father hired a company called Pinkerton to investigate Tookov in America. Find out what you can about them. I'll be doing the same in the First-Class lounge. Here's a map of America to help you orient yourself. It's a huge country and Arkansas seems to be in the middle, right enough."

Tam's eyes gleamed. Truth be told, he was bored in Ballboyne and this adventure seemed tailor-made for him: travel, intrigue, Danger, new customs, new people, (and new women). *Adds spice to life, doesn't it?* he thought to himself.

"Mr. Rennie, how shall I tell you if I find anything of importance?"

"As I understand it, the one place the first and second-class passengers mingle is in the Smoking Room after dinner. Meet me there after dinner every night and report."

And so the adventure started.

End of Part 1

Part II

"The wide world is all before us -
but a world without a friend"

Strathallan's Lament

Robert Burns

Chapter 13

Another early morning, another day of excitement and promise, another warm day with temperatures in the high 50s and a clear sky. The winds of yesterday had blown the smoke from the iron works off to the east. The Gordons were up and about at dawn, getting ready to go to the steamship office for their medical examinations. They took turns washing in the basin set on the table in the corner of their room. George kept busy running up and down the stairs to fill the crockery pitcher with water from the tap in the kitchen. He managed two mugs of hot water so he and his Da could shave.

Mrs. Duncan fed them well with homemade scones to go with their porridge and milk. A cup of hot, sweet tea rounded off the breakfast.

"Mrs. Duncan?" asked Harry. "Can you tell us how to get to Bothwell Street?"

"Ah, you're going on the Stewart Steamship Line. Having our medical exam today, are we?" No secrets here, it's as though they had a big tattoo on their foreheads saying "Emigrants". "It's only a mile away, an easy walk on a fine day like this. You're right to get there early, there'll be a big queue later." Mrs. Duncan gave them clear and explicit directions

Harry looked resplendent in his three-piece suit, a brown tweed with cap to match. He'd had his suit since his wedding 25 years before, a testament to the cloth's durability, the infrequency with which he wore it and his own high metabolic rate which kept his weight stable. Truth be told, he only put the suit on for 'hatches', 'matches' and 'dispatches' as he called births, weddings and funerals. It's outdated style and baggy knees bothered him not one little bit. The starched, detachable shirt collar was fashionable though, a recent investment because his last shirt and collar had succumbed to old age. His cream cravat and gold-plated tie pin were still old-school, he'd had them forever. He wore brown boots, dazzling, polished right up to the ankle, ideal for avoiding the rubbish prevalent on the streets of Glasgow.

His wife wore a demure mid-grey woolen dress. To fill out the scoop at her neck, she wore a white cotton dickey with hand-stitched pink roses on the chin-high collar, crisp and spotless despite having been in her valise for a day. She wore the bonnet she had stitched with roses and matching ribbons. The ever-present breeze required her to drape a gray shawl over her shoulders.

Bella had dressed in a similar fashion, high laced boots with a wee heel, long black dress and a white high-necked blouse trimmed with lace. Her prize possession, her grandmother's honey-colored cairngorm pin set in a sensuous Celtic-inspired setting, held together her Gordon tartan shawl. A saucy little bonnet trimmed with a sprig of white heather topped her off. She was most respectable, yet her infectious excitement bubbled through and, with her flashing smile and bright eyes, she'd have stood out in a crowd even if she'd only worn a tatty sack!

And then there was George. Oh my, George! He wore the formal dress of his old regiment, the Black Watch, and looked magnificent! His black boots were mirror-polished and threatened to outshine the sun, however the white spats were ill-designed for the Glasgow streets. He'd have to pick his way through the muck and mire with care. His white hose with the red crosshatching were immaculate, as were the red flashes to keep them from sliding down to his ankles. His kilt sported the Black Watch tartan of course, black and dark green, somber, sober, substantial, no flighty reds or yellows here. This was a full kilt, eight yards of heavy wool and warm enough to keep the wearer content on the coldest nights. The stone in his kilt pin also came from the Cairngorms, a darker shade of amber than Bella's brooch, set in silver. His protective sporran came from the finest leather and hung over his front, more utilitarian than many. His jacket made up for it, a magnificent hunting red with gold piping on the collar as a counterpoint to the black velvet cuffs. He had two sashes, one of white canvas which held his ceremonial ammunition pouch, and a decorative one of deep red across the opposite shoulder. The black Glengarry hat he wore sported the silver regimental badge with the regiment's motto "Nemo Me Impune Lacessit" or "No One Provokes Me with Impunity". Topping this glorious pageantry fluttered the "Red Heckle", a red feather awarded to the regiment after an audacious rescue of two field artillery pieces abandoned by an English regiment, the Grenadiers, in Holland in 1794.

Harry viewed George with satisfaction and envy. He was proud of the man his son had become, confident, competent, seasoned. However, he envied George his dramatic appearance. Harry turned to Fiona and sighed. "Doesn't George look imposing?! I wish I could wear a kilt but I'd appear ridiculous. With my boney legs and scrawny body, I'd look like a roll of tartan with two pipe-cleaners hanging down!"

Fiona laughed. "You're right there! I'm not sure anyone might call you impressive!"

They arrived at the Stewart Shipping Line's offices after a thirty-minute walk, Bella gawking around in a most unladylike way, taking in the new sights, sounds and, sad to say, smells. Much busier than Aberdeen, the pedestrians shunted her onto the road more than once. George noticed her dilemma and suggested, "Come behind me!" With his height, bulk and sheer presence, the people parted like a biblical miracle and Bella walked safe in his wake.

The basement of the Stewart Line building housed the office for the steerage class emigrants' medicals. It was a low, dingy room with bench seating for forty people in the middle with additional benches round the sides for another twenty. The air was stuffy, stale and smelled rank, the evidence of cigarettes, pipes and ripe bodies lingering long after their owners left. Despite their early arrival, the Gordons were relegated to seats on a side bench where they sat and waited, and waited, and waited.

The different accents and even languages fascinated Bella. She was constantly nudging George in the ribs. "George, where are those people from?" She nodded toward the latest couple to catch her ear.

"I don't understand the language. They may be Scandinavian. They're blonde enough." Their spotless multi-colored clothing, rosy cheeks and general air of well-being set them apart from the rest of the emigrants.

"How about them? I love their accent."

"By the sound of them, they're from Wales."

Bella and George examined them with interest, no malice in their scrutiny. It was a family of four, father, mother and two little girls. The father was short and powerful with clean though old clothes. Nothing, however, could scour the coal dust from his eyes and hands. George would have bet money he was a miner. The wife had the air of the near-defeated, no color in her cheeks, no life in her voice, no pride in her clothes. She sat as though in shock, staring at the floor between her boots. Even the children were spiritless. Bella judged them to be seven and nine, an age where they should have been causing noise, havoc and mischief, however they too sat motionless and apathetic. The eldest little girl stretched out her hand to her ma and Bella noticed the arm above the hand was rail-thin. All came clear to Bella in an instant. "They're starving! Ma, is there any food left from yesterday?"

"The one jam roll neither of you wanted, Bella. Why?"

"Let me have it please."

Fiona rummaged through her bag and pulled out the remaining roll, still in the paper bag and much the worse for wear. Bella split it in two halves and took them to the two young lassies.

"Here, take this."

The young girls gawked at the half roll, peeked at Bella, looked at their Ma, stared at the sandwich again with naked hunger in their eyes.

The father protested they couldn't accept charity but the mother cut him short. "Evan Morgan, the girls are starving, we have no money so they will eat nothing until we get on board. This once, we will accept what the good Lord offers no matter how He offers it." She turned to the girls. "What do you say, now?"

In unison, the girls turned to Bella and said, "Thank you, Miss!" Then they fell on their half roll and demolished it to a crumb.

Every few minutes, the clerk in the wicket window called "Next" and the person or the family in the first seats of the front row rose and approached the agent. Then the 'shuffle' began, everyone taking turns to shuffle along the benches towards the front row and their turn in front of the clerk. Woe betide anyone who tried to jump ahead! A chorus of catcalls would shame them into returning to their rightful place. It took an hour of shuffling before the Gordons progressed even to the inner square of benches.

"What are they doing, George? Why is it taking so long?" Bella of course.

"I don't know, Bella. You'll have to be patient." This from an ex-soldier inured to hurrying up and waiting.

A young man in his early twenties, clean, sober, well-dressed, and presentable, sat alone behind George's back. He had curly black hair, thick muttonchops, and good teeth which he displayed in a winning grin whenever he got the chance.

"Pardon me, sir." He turned to address George but he fooled no-one, it was Bella he wanted to impress. "I couldn't help but overhear the young lady's question." His accent revealed an Ulster man. "I've been through here before and I'd be happy to explain today's process to you. Allow me to introduce myself, my name's James Webb." Again, the grin for Bella's benefit. Little did he know he was wasting his time. Since meeting Sir David, Bella was immune to other men's charms, however she was thirsty for more news of what the family could expect, and nudged George to accept the offer.

"Good to meet you, Mr. Webb, my name is Gordon. Thank you, sir, that would be helpful. You said you'd been through here already. How so?"

"This is my third time in this office. I first emigrated four years ago, then again two years past. I live in Atlantic City, 120 miles south of New York. I work there in the winter and go back home to Lurgan for the summer when I can."

Bella found this breathtaking. Here was someone who not only had made the voyage before, but had accomplished it three times! And how much money did he have to make to afford the fare? And how did he make a living? Questions kept bubbling up but the Irishman was still talking to George.

"There are two inspections one must undergo here, Mr. Gordon. Failure in either one may mean you won't get on your ship. The agent at the wicket there," he nodded towards the clerk, "is inspecting the paperwork and tickets for completeness and accuracy. Many people prepay only a part of their fare so he collects the balance. He also gives you a form to fill out, which he discusses with each of you. He'll ask questions to make sure you were truthful with your answers."

"What kind of questions?" Bella was irrepressible.

James Webb laughed, "Stupid questions, really! Questions like are you a bigamist, or an anarchist, or a felon! Who in their right mind would answer 'Yes!'?"

George also found Mr. Webb interesting. "Are there many people such as yersel' who come back from America?"

"Oh, yes, when I came over last June, women and children on the ten-pound cure almost filled the boat."

"What's the ten-pound cure?"

"Well, we Irish find it difficult to get work, we're discriminated against something fierce. It'll be easier for you being Scottish and all. When a man does get a job, he also gets a circle of friends, or at least mates he can have a pint of beer with after work."

Bella nodded her understanding.

The Irishman continued. "His wife gets stuck at home with the kids and has a tough time meeting people and making friends herself. She misses her ma and Da and remembers her home with a fondness it rarely warrants. So once the family gets their feet under them, she agitates for the family to return. However, the wise man spends the ten pounds to send her back by herself."

"You mean the family breaks up?" Bella was aghast.

Webb laughed again. "Not often! The wife gets home and suddenly remembers the reasons she left in first place, be it living conditions or lack of work or the bloody English. Or how she doesn't get along with her Ma, which she has managed to blot from her memory! Her lot in America won't be peaches and cream, nonetheless she has the promise of a much better life. She uses the last half of the return ticket to go back to her man in America."

"Yes!" thought Bella. "It's the 'Promise' we're chasing!"

"You mentioned two inspections, is the other one the medical?" George became engrossed in his conversation, Harry and Fiona were trying hard not to be obvious about their eavesdropping.

"Yes, again it's pretty cursory. It's a surprise they even bother. Anyone the US Government finds unfit at the inspection in America is sent back at the steamship company's expense so the company must at least appear to be inspecting us. They'll check your teeth and eyes. They might listen to your heart too and that's it!"

The Gordons had a dozen other questions but the clerk called for the next family and the 'shuffle' took them away from Mr. Webb, leaving them awash with their thoughts.

The mood was tense. This was a most important hurdle for the emigrants. Harry realized the Gordons might learn something from their predecessors.

"Watch carefully, see what happens so we're prepared when our turn comes."

Harry sorted the family birth certificates and application forms and manifests for each member of the family in the order he saw the agent examine them. *Make it easy for them to pass us on, don't give them a reason to turn us back.* he thought to himself.

Soon after the family separated from Mr. Webb, the agent did just that, turned a family back. There was six of them, Pa, Ma and four little ones ranging in age from eight to two. They appeared to be farmers, or at least farm laborers They seemed healthy and well-fed however their patched clothes and unkempt hair led Bella to believe their farm was unsuccessful.

"What do you mean, we can't go on board?" The father shouted at the top of his voice. The agent whispered something which infuriated the farmer even more. "Come back next week?! What are we to do till then? You've got to let us on board!" And he climbed onto the counter to get to the agent. It looked like trouble then a door opened behind the Gordons and two brawny men rushed in to drag the farmer away. The agent didn't even blink. *This must be a common occurrence.* thought Bella. In the meantime, the farmer's wife was shrieking at him. “It’s all your fault, you miserable excuse for a man! You couldn’t organize a piss-up at a brewery. I should have listened to my mother and never married you …” And she would have gone on and on but the bairns were now in full voice and she had to choose between berating him or comforting them. At last, the parents found common ground. “Where are we to go from here? How do we get back home?” The man looked like a rabbit in front of a weasel, paralyzed, faced with decisions he was ill-equipped to make.

The farm family left, shoulders sagging, heads down, shuffling their feet up the stairs to the street. The high tension rubbed off on the waiting émigrés who huddled closer and whispered softer amongst themselves.

The families successful in navigating the maze of bureaucratic paperwork disappeared into rooms behind the clerk. Ten minutes later, they emerged waving the stamped documents in their hands, relief obvious on their faces. Little did they know the hardest part was yet to come, the transatlantic crossing.

#

At last, four hours after they had arrived at the steamship offices, the Gordons were in the premium seats in the front row. The office had filled, all the seats taken, families queuing up the stairs and spilling into the street. The noise level remained subdued as though the emigrants didn’t want to draw disapproval from the agent. The Gordons’ turn came at last and they approached the agent with a mixture of excitement and trepidation. The clerk was in his mid-twenties, the epitome of an 'ink-stained wretch'. Pale, as though he never rose above ground, bony, as though he never got enough to eat, and unhealthy, his sniffling and coughing marking him as an early candidate for consumption. His clothes were hand-me-downs from a much larger man, creased and crumpled around his scrawny frame. Perched on the end of a sharp nose were a pair of wire-rimmed spectacles which had seen better days. Bella dubbed him 'The Mole'.

"Papers, please." The Mole's voice was an octave deeper than expected and lent an air of authority he didn't possess with his mouth closed. Harry laid out the papers in their order, one pile for each Gordon. The clerk nodded to Harry in appreciation. He had seen too many heads of families come to his wicket in utter disarray.

"Which of you is …" he squinted at the birth certificate on top of the first pile, "Harold Milne Gordon?"

"I am, sir."

The inquisition began, one family member at a time. The Mole's boredom was evident, only when he was talking to Bella did he show any interest in the family in front of him. He asked each of them to verify the answers they had given to the twenty questions on the application form. The Gordons satisfied The Mole none of them were insane or infirm, bigamists, anarchists or paupers, they had enough money to get them to their destination and so wouldn't become wards of the state, and their destination included a relative. The Mole checked the birth certificates against the tickets and the ship's manifest, ensured the Gordon's had paid their fares in full and nodded them through to the room behind him.

The Gordons exhaled as if they had been holding their breath for hours. "Well, so far, thon Irishman has proven to be accurate, not much trouble there. I hope the medical exam is as easy." Harry showed uncharacteristic excitement.

The examining room was small and cramped for the four of them, airless and humid. As Fiona sat in the sole chair, she noticed dirt in the corners and under the sideboards containing medical instruments and supplies. She didn't have time to protest because the doctor came bustling in and sat at the desk. He seemed much too young, short, stocky and good tempered with carrot-red hair and a black, blue and purple shiner. "A rugby player." thought George.

"I'm Doctor Charles." He said by way of introduction. "And you are …" he checked the papers, "the Gordon family. Off to America, are we?"

"Yes, sir." answered Harry. "California."

"I hear it's beautiful there, hot though, very different than Bonnie Scotland, eh!?" He turned to business. "Right! I'll need you to tell me your medical history, then I'll give you a quick once over. Mr. Gordon, you first."

Dr. Charles checked Harry's physical and mental history which seemed satisfactory, then started the examination. He concentrated first on Harry's eyes, searching for any sign of trachoma, then his teeth. He checked Harry's heart and lungs with a stethoscope then invited Harry to walk a few steps in the crowded little room, checking for any infirmity. And that was it! Dr. Charles stamped Harry's boarding pass and moved on to George, same process, same result. Next came Fiona, almost the same process, same result. The difference was the good doctor enquired about her monthly cycle which embarrassed Fiona no end, to have to discuss such matters with a man, in front of men. Harry saw his wife's discomfort and suggested he and George leave the room while the good doctor examined Bella, her mother staying as chaperone. The men left, the examination continued, then Fiona and Bella too emerged triumphant.

The Gordon family reunited outside the examination room and couldn't contain their excitement, hugs between the women, handshakes for the men, then up the stairs to daylight, fresh air and the promise of freedom.

On the top steps of the steamship line's entrance sat the farming family who 'The Mole' had turned back. The parents had retreated into a shocked, catatonic state, the children, sensing the looming disaster, were quietly waiting. Harry saw them first and knelt by the father to see if he could help.

The farmer regarded him with hopeless, terrified eyes. "They won't let us on!" He had a Borders accent, a shepherd, then, not a farmer.

"Why not?" Harry's calm voice eased the shepherd's distress.

"There's something missing from our papers! I don't know what, I'm not much schooled!"

Harry remembered sorting his family's papers and could quite understand something going astray. "If you wish, I could study them and see if I can figure out what's amiss."

The shepherd turned to his wife for support but none came. She still stared of into space, distilling anger from every pore. He shook himself and decided. “All right, Mister. Don’t go running off with them or I’ll stomp you!” He produced a wad of papers from his jacket pocket and handed them over to Harry.

Harry sorted the papers by individual, then put the papers into the same order Harry had presented to the Mole. “There’s one piece of paper missing. It’s the birth certificate for … “He squinted at one of the piles. “Helen. Is it in another pocket perhaps?”

The shepherd patted and poked and prodded various parts of his body, his breast pocket, his back pocket, even his coin pockets with increasing apprehension. “I’ve seen it, it’s got to be here somewhere, Alice, have you seen it?”

His wife reacted as though an electric current had passed through her.

“Oh God, Bob, I have seen it. It’s right here in my bag. I used it to help teach Morag to read while on the train here yesterday. Oh, this my fault. Bob, I’m so sorry for calling you those names. It was my fault. I’ve been so angry at having to leave Langholm I stopped listening and vented on you.” She rooted through her bag, found the birth certificate and passed it over to him.

Bella examined the shepherd to see what effect his wife’s contrition was having on him. Not much! Bella figured an awful lot of atonement would have to happen before this became a happy family again.

The shepherd turned to Harry. "What do we do now? Can we get in line again?"

"I expect so, though it's getting late in the day, you may have to come back tomorrow."

"That we can do. Sir, I'll never be able to repay you, I am in your debt."

"Nonsense, sir. I wish you and your family Godspeed."

The Gordon's headed back to Mrs. Duncan's, changed into their travelling clothes and packed their Sunday best into their trunks. They were starving. "My!" said Harry, "Breakfast was an awful long time ago. I saw a fish and chip shop around the corner, how about we share a couple o' fish suppers?"

Chapter 14

David and Tam had endured a whirling dervish of a week so found the train trip in the first-class carriage to Glasgow relaxing. The Aberdeen Station was busier than wee Ballboyne, with its usual mix of business, upper crust and even family passengers. Military lads lazed about, well-trained in doing nothing.

"Those are the uniforms of an English regiment, the Grenadier Guards." Tam noted.

"They must guard the Royal Family at Balmoral Castle," said David, "I saw several at the Ballboyne station."

As the train steamed south, David and Tam talked about the known, the unknown, the might-be-known for most of their journey. David took much advantage of the older man's organizational skills and his experience in sorting the wheat from the chaff, while David impressed Tam by his speed of learning and his intuitive ability to put together pieces of this puzzle.

David had thought long and hard about the likelihood of being able to salvage his family's fortune and decided he didn't like the odds. He also realized doing nothing was not an option, his family's honor was at stake and he could never live with himself if his family lost everything and he hadn't done his utmost to prevent it. His next steps were easy, get to America and find a trail to follow.

David and Tam parted ways when the train arrived at Queen Street Station. Tam headed to the Port of Glasgow docks with their luggage while David met with his father's solicitor, Fergus Cameron and James Drysdale, the accountant. Their meeting was to take place in Cameron's office in a fine stone building at the east end of Glasgow's Sauchiehall Street. Clutching his briefcase of papers, David had walked from the railway station, a decision he regretted the first time he had to cross a manure-thick road. He knocked the sharn off his shoes and ran up the stairs to the second-floor offices, glad of the exercise, and found himself in what he described to Tam later as a fire trap. Cameron's office had bundles of papers tied up with thin pink ribbons stacked to the ceiling. There were also dozens of light blue cardboard boxes, closed with similar pink restraints, lined up along the walls. Cameron shook David's hand and offered him a seat before realizing all the seats were covered with client files. He moved a pile onto the floor, releasing a veritable whirlwind of dust as he did so. Cameron flapped his hands, which spread the motes to the further corners of the room and initiated a series of violent sneezes. David took the proffered chair anyway, wondering how the solicitor could ever find a file when needed.

Drysdale arrived soon after and performed the same ceremonial greeting, file moving, seating and sneezing. Cameron offered a glass of whisky which gave David a chance to observe each of them. Fergus Cameron was sandy and bristly, sandy because of the straw-colored hair and fair skin, bristly because of his short-clipped military mustache and air of aggressive defensiveness. James Drysdale appeared quieter, more thoughtful, spare of speech. He was dark and slim, well-groomed where Cameron seemed disordered as though he had no wife to keep him sharp. The obligatory small talk centered on which local soccer team, Rangers or Celtic, would prevail in next Saturday's derby. David tried to hide his impatience.

"Gentlemen, I'm booked on a boat leaving this evening, let's get down to business, shall we?" Although couched as a request, both professionals recognized a command when they heard one.

"In the interests of expediency, let me summarize what I know, then you can correct me or fill any gaps in my knowledge." Heads nodded in agreement, the accountant and solicitor glancing at each other and wondering about this young man, a force to be reckoned with by the sound of things. Unease spread across their faces. David saw it and said "I'm not interested in pointing fingers, I need to make sure I know everything pertinent so I can catch Tookov and get our money back. We must work together for that." Cameron and Drysdale relaxed, sitting back in their chairs, although they hung onto every word as David laid out all he had learned. "What have I missed?"

The two professionals looked at each other and shrugged. "Nothing, Sir David, your summary of the situation matches the facts as I know them!" Cameron, eager to please.

Drysdale, thoughtful as ever, concurred "I agree Sir David, but may I make a point. You're off to America to do what, exactly? Apprehend Tookov? You don't have the authority. Beat the money out of him?" Drysdale smiled at his own jest, then smothered it when he saw David didn't share his amusement. "Umm, it's obvious Mr. Cameron and I wish you to bring this Tookov to justice and to recover as much of our investment as possible. I don't much care what this justice looks like, you can tie the bastard to an anthill and cover him in honey if you wish! It's all the same to me."

Cameron jumped in with a suggestion or two of his own, which included snake pits, sharks, alligators and buzzards. David had trouble hiding his amusement at the criminal inventiveness of these two pillars of Glasgow society.

Drysdale brought them back to earth with another sage comment. "Might I suggest, Sir David, one of your first tasks is to confirm Lord Rennie, Mr. Cameron and myself are indeed the rightful owners of the mine? You will have seen the papers suggesting this but they are American documents and I can't say whether they are accurate, complete or forgeries. I don't know who the authority would be to confirm their authenticity, perhaps there's a Federal Department of Mines."

David nodded to Drysdale with renewed appreciation. "The thought had struck me too, I'm meeting with the British Consul General in New York when I arrive. He'll be able to point me in the right direction. You should also know my father has sold his share of the mine to me to expedite any dealings I may need to make. Mr. Cameron, please make sure my father and I have signed the appropriate document in the appropriate places."

Cameron looked at Drysdale, a 21-year-old now owned their investment! They chewed this over for a moment then Drysdale gave a slight nod. David's take-charge demeanor impressed him, and, in reality, he had no other option.

The three of them talked for another hour but they were going over the same ground. David realized these gentlemen were not to blame for his family's financial fiasco and came to appreciate their expert opinion on both the legal and the monetary aspects. Finally, he accepted them as equal partners in a disastrous enterprise.

He took his leave of the two, their good wishes more in hope than expectation, and bounded down the stairs to the street, eager to get to his ship. Businesses were closing, the street crowded with homebound workers who shouldered and shoved him for he seemed to be going against the flow of humanity. He had not gone a block when someone jostled him in the back, then dragged him into a dark, narrow alleyway. David struggled back and elbowed his attacker hard on the side of the head. He heard a shout of pain and a flow of curses then something heavy smashed into his head, just behind his ear. He dropped like a sack of potatoes, lying there in the rubbish and dirt, defenseless, helpless. His attacker booted him twice, then there were more voices and shouts, a nearby voice said, "Keep away from America!" and his assailant ran off. Stunned by the assault, David lay still. Next thing he knew, he was being questioned by a circle of interested bystanders.

"Hey, are you all right Mac? Boy, someone done you good and proper, what was they after?" David found the almost impenetrable Glasgow accent comforting.

Good question. thought David. He still had his briefcase so robbery wasn't the motive. *Ah yes,* he remembered, *Keep away from America*, a warning…or worse. What would have transpired if the Good Samaritans hadn't showed up? "What happened?" he asked.

"Thon soldier beat you up was what happened." said the self-appointed ringleader of his rescuers, a large, overweight but hard man, a dock worker perhaps, dressed in khaki overalls and big brown boots and wearing a black leather cap.

"A soldier?" David puzzled, "What uniform?"

"I dunno, Mac, don't know nuthin' about those Guards blokes. Although I did see somethin' on his cap, a bloody hand grenade! He was a corporal, had the two stripes on his sleeve."

David struggled to his feet and thanked his rescuers by giving them a pound to buy themselves a drink, an offer accepted with delight. He hailed a hansom cab to take him to the Port of Glasgow, arriving in plenty of time to catch the small tender out to the SS Curambria. After the formalities of ticketing and shipping manifests were complete, David asked a steward to bring Tam to his cabin. When Tam arrived, and heard of David's assault, he was aghast.

"Are you all right, Sire?!" Tam's lapse back into formality seemed most appropriate.

"Yes, a big lump on the back of my head and an even bigger headache, but I'll be fine. The question is, who was my attacker, how did he know where I was, and what did he want to accomplish?"

Tam thought for a moment. "Well, in reverse order, it sounds like he wanted to scare you off from America. And perhaps more than scare you off, if the Good Samaritans as you call them hadn't arrived on the scene, he might have done a lot more and a lot worse to you."

David digested this unpleasant thought. "You're right, the arrival of the Samaritans frustrated him, he was cursing like a fishwife when he ran off."

"What accent?"

"What? Oh, I see, it was English, East London, I think. It fits, doesn't it? A Grenadier Guardsman … "

"Wait!" Tam interrupted. "A Grenadier?"

"Sorry, Tam, I forgot to tell you my rescuer said he saw a grenade badge on the attacker's cap. And it was the Grenadiers we saw at the Ballboyne station and the Aberdeen station." David followed his thought. "Suppose Thomas/Tookov detailed this soldier to keep an ear open for any activity at Castle Cranach.

Tam interrupted. "It would have been easy for him to find out about our plan to go to America, our travel plans were the talk of the village. First, he takes a shot at you by the bridge, using a rifle. Then he shadows us from Ballboyne to

Glasgow, follows you to Cameron's offices, waits and jumps you when you leave."

"Yes, sounds about right. But isn't he absent without leave?"

"Yes, he is, but perhaps his usefulness is over in Ballboyne, perhaps we'll see him again in America. I really, really hope we do!" Tam flexed his fists, he had 'the look' in his eye.

David hesitated, fingering the back of his head, "Tam, how well do you know Mrs. Forbes, the postmistress in Ballboyne?"

Tam cracked a grin. "Not as well as you might imagine, Mr. Rennie, but well enough"

"Then I want you to send a telegram to her as soon as possible. I want to know the name of any corporal in the barracks at Ballboyne who has been receiving telegrams from America. And I want to know where they came from in America."

"Yes sir!" Tam all but saluted. "Now, if there's nothing else, I suggest you change for dinner, nothing like a full stomach to sooth your aches and pains."

"Thank you, Mother Hen!"

Chapter 15

The SS Curambria waltzed at anchor in the middle of the Firth of Clyde's seaway. It was a cold, bright morning with an icy wind from the north, cold enough to bring roses to the cheeks of those watching the tender bringing the last of the steerage class passengers from shore. David was one onlooker, nursing his bruises by idling against the rail on the First-Class passengers' deck and trying to make sense of the sailors' activities as they prepared the ship for sailing. It looked like chaos, an anthill overturned, it even sounded like bedlam with the Officers shouting orders to the crew and the crew shouting at each other, all interspersed with long, loud blasts from the ship's foghorn.

He shifted his gaze to the other First-Class passengers who would be his travel companions for the next ten days. They were a good slice of the British population, many upper class but a fair sprinkling of the middle class too. He recognized a dozen different accents, south of England, Welsh, north, south, east and west coast Scots, Geordies, even a few Irish, and a surprising number of Americans returning home. At dinner last night, he had made the acquaintance of a couple from Boston, two businessmen from New York and a timber baron from Georgia with whom he had discussed new forestry methods. Tam was visible on the Second-Class deck, at ease at the rail and already in deep conversation with an attractive woman in her mid-thirties. David smiled. *It was ever thus!* he thought. Tam later introduced her as Mrs. Hamm, a widow lady.

The tender had hooked on to the Curambria and the immigrants were coming aboard. David turned away, not noticing the puzzlement and disbelief on the upturned face of a young lassie on the tender, one Bella Gordon. David had crossed to the other side of the deck and was admiring the Rosneath Peninsula a few miles over the water to the west. He took a deep breath, savoring the crisp sea air, and allowed himself to relax.

After dinner that night, he and Tam met in the Smoking Lounge as planned. "Anything to report?" David enquired.

"Oh yes, Mr. Rennie, oh yes!" Tam had the gleam in his eye normally reserved for the ladies. "I got a reply from Mrs. Forbes. She says there has been considerable correspondence between America and one Corporal Michael Thomas of the Grenadier Guards!"

"Thomas, eh?! Perhaps a relative of Tookov?"

"Maybe so, sir, maybe so."

"Where have the telegrams come from?"

"They seem to come every week. The first one came from New York about three months ago, soon after the Grenadiers arrived in Ballboyne for duty. Then there was the one from the American capital, Washington. But there's been a flurry of telegrams this last week, all coming from St. Louis, Missouri, which, by the way, is right next to Arkansas."

"So Pinkertons may be right, Tookov is on his way to Rush to tie up loose ends. Thank you, Tam!"

They stared at each other, each aware of their heightened pulse rate, excited to know they were on the right track.

"Mrs. Forbes didn't read any of the latest telegrams by chance?"

"Oh no, Mr. Rennie, she wouldn't involve herself in anything illegal…though she did say they appeared to be in code."

Little did they know the last telegram from St. Louis said:

"USE ALL MEANS REPEAT ALL MEANS POSSIBLE PREVENT RENNIE'S SON FROM REACHING AMERICA STOP"

David smiled. "Bless Mrs. Forbes! Is there any way to thank her for her help?"

Tam thought for a moment, "Aye, she wants to build a new house on land she owns near Ballboyne and is having trouble getting the right permission because one of her neighbors is objecting. Perhaps Lord Rennie could have a word?"

"Send a telegram in my name to my father, I'm sure he'd love to 'have a word'!"

Chapter 16

Bella and family were listening to Sandy McLean, the bagpiper, as he strolled up and down the Port of Glasgow dock. He was playing a medley of jigs and reels and marches, festive music for the festive occasion. Like George the day before, Sandy stepped out in full dress fig, Tam o' Shanter crammed onto his head, McLean tartan kilt skirting his knees, black velvet Prince Charlie jacket snug around his shoulders, sgian dubh, his ceremonial dagger, peeking out of his green hose. They say "clothes maketh the man" but it was his bulk which gave him the gravitas, grandeur and authority. Let's be kind and say he was stocky, 5' 6" of broad chest and bum, propped up on legs like ham hocks. Sandy had played here for years, hired by the steamship companies to give the emigrants a fitting sendoff to the New World.

Passengers and relatives and well-wishers crowded the dock, aye, and touts and charlatans, selling sea-sick remedies and whisky, almost interchangeably. It was easy to tell who was passenger and who was relative by their body language and demeanor. Most of the émigrés were in a holiday mood, excited by the adventure, impatient to say the final goodbyes and to get underway. The relatives were glum, with sagging shoulders, brave face and a determination not to cry. Bella, ever a people-watcher, watched the interplay within the families. The Wilsons were a case in point. Jimmy Wilson, the patriarch, was short, dark and wiry, an intense man and not one many people crossed. Friday night drunks had found to their dismay ferocity had nothing to do with size. He was one of Glasgow's 'hard men', yet here he was, struggling with knowing his daughter Moira was about to leave him for good. Snatches of conversation revealed other powerful undercurrents plaguing him.

"I'm right sad to see you go, lassie, and that's a fact. But I like your chances, you'll hae more opportunities there in America. Britain'll never change. I should have done it maself twenty years ago but I didnae hae the bottle to leave. I'm sad, but I'm proud of you too."

Then Jimmy turned and walked up the pier, his wife Maggie scampering after him like a Scottie at dinnertime. Jimmy's voice rose. Anger and its flip side fear roiled below the surface. "You know, Maggie, that could hae been us, you know. That could hae been us 20 years ago! But we were frightened, I was frightened. And now life is passing us by." He glanced back at Moira, the battle between pride and sadness showing on his face. Jimmy felt a limb of his family tree was being ripped off for transplanting.

The weather had changed again, a cold, windy day with the smell of winter about it. The salty tang of the ocean sharpened the senses, the seagulls keened a white-noise constant in the background. The frothy white clouds scudded by for all the world like the sailing ships of yore.

Bella and her Ma walked up and down the dock to keep warm while waiting to board the Curambria. Bella shivered.

"Are you all right my dear?" Fiona had noticed. "We'll be aboard soon. But there's more, isn't there?"

Bella sighed. "Yes, Ma, there's more. I know it's foolish but I can't get Sir David out of my head. As busy as we've been the past few days, his face keeps popping into my mind."

"Ah lassie, you've got it bad, so you have. It's sad you never got to know him better, he seemed like a good man. You know, my dear, first romances are always special and often painful. And there's no cure known to man nor beast. Time and distance will heal everything, my dear, you canna dwell on it."

"I know that in my mind, Ma, but try telling my heart!" A cloud crossed her face. "I'll be all right. We'll just need to keep me busy!"

It was time for the passengers to board the small tender, the Caledonia, which was to ferry them out to the SS Curambria. The relatives wailed their final tears, the emigrants said their last good byes, they were underway. Sandy the piper came along on the Caledonia and continued playing up-tempo jigs and strathspeys. Bella and family were amongst the other emigrants, facing the shore, waving to the remaining well-wishers, whether known or not, until they could no longer identify them as individuals. Then, as one, they pivoted to the steamship still ahead of them, to look forward to new lives, to turn their backs on the old one. Sandy saw his cue and started to play laments, slow, sad, mournful tunes intended to tug at the heartstrings and to raise the emotional temperature. This was by design. Before one can heal, one must grieve. Soon, everyone, the adventurers and the young mums, the settlers and the travelers, was in tears, racked with sobs and heaving shoulders … yes, even the Scottish men!

As the Caledonia approached the Curambria, Bella saw the crew had draped a stairway over the side and was standing at the bottom to help the newcomers transition from the tender to the Curambria. The travelers put their first foot forward onto the steps taking them to a new life. They changed from being emigrants to immigrants.

While waiting her turn, Bella scanned the faces of the passengers already on board and lining the decks watching the newcomers. Her heart skipped a beat. *Wasn't that ..., couldn't be, what would Sir David be doing here!* She craned her neck to see but the man in question, high up on the first-class passengers' deck, had turned away. She laughed at herself. *What a foolish notion!* But the thought of David saddened her again and distracted her. So much so she almost missed her step and would have ended up in the drink were it not for the strong arm of a sailor. Bella thanked him, removed his hand from her bosom then slapped him for taking liberties with her while saving her. She didn't notice the gleam of appreciation on the face of the ship's officer supervising the boarding process.

"Second class or steerage?" A sailor checked their names on the manifest. "Ah yes, Mr. and Mrs. Gordon, please follow this sailor to the married quarters. Mr. George Gordon, this sailor will take you to the single gentlemen's berths.' He managed to avoid sneering at the word 'gentleman'. "Miss Gordon, you'll be in the single ladies' room for'ard."

"You mean we're not to be together?" Fiona was apprehensive, and was right to be so.

"No, miss. But you'll be able to be together anytime except for sleeping. I suggest you settle into your berths and meet, oh, in an hour in the dining area."

Mollified, the Gordons went their separate ways. The ship's officer stepped forward and offered to take Bella's valise. "Let me help you find your quarters, Miss." Bella saw nothing irregular in an officer volunteering for a seaman's duty. The officer led the way through a maze of ill-lit passageways and hatches, stopping to help Bella over the coaming each time, and each time becoming more forward by touching her hand, arm or body. Bella was growing alarmed, she would never find her way back to her family and became apprehensive about the officer's familiarity. At last, the officer opened a door saying, "Here we are!" Bella was about to refuse to enter but saw the room already occupied by women, most of them young. The cabin seemed large but crowded as it held about twenty bunks packed together like sardines in a can. Bella couldn't make out the empty bunks because the only light came from two portholes on the far side of the room. The officer squeezed his way around the bunks to the bulkhead and hoisted Bella's valise onto the topmost bunk under one porthole. "Here we are Miss Gordon, you'll be snug as a bug here. I'll drop by to make sure you're all right later."

Once he was out of the room and out of earshot, there was a chorus of jeers and catcalls directed at Bella.

"Captain Casanova has found his bed-warmer for the trip!" laughed a young Irishwoman named Kate. She had the soft brogue of the west coast, County Clare perhaps.

"What do you mean?" Bella didn't appreciate the comment.

"That scum's chosen you to meet his needs this trip. His name is Wilhelm Lederbeiter and he'll pursue you until he has you in his bed and he'll stop at nothing until he succeeds. He's the authority on this deck and beyond. He says he can get you deported from America if you don't play his games."

Bella blanched. She thought about his over-familiarity on their trip through steerage, it all fitted. "That's why he was so helpful. But how do you know this?"

Kate took pity on the young Scots lassie. Her voice softened. "Because I was on the Curambria three years past when I first came to America and watched him in action. He's a pig!"

"Were you …?"

"Was I his bedmate? No. I wasn't young enough or innocent enough or bonnie enough. But I could still see what he was up to. He was panting after a young, innocent colleen from western Ireland, she was just fifteen. We tried to keep her safe but he found a way to get to her." Kate's eyes clouded over in sorrow. "The poor wee thing jumped overboard in shame." There was a collective intake of breath from the assembled women. Kate looked at Bella, a sad and sympathetic expression on her face. "And you, my dear, look just like her." Bella's hand went to her throat and she took a step back. She felt faint and her knees wobbled for a moment. She grabbed onto the side of a bunk until she righted herself.

One woman, older than most, late-twenties perhaps, showed an intense interest in Kate's story. "Do you remember the name of the girl?" An American accent.

"Yes, Brigid Murphy. She was from County Galway, almost a neighbor of mine. I'll never forget her. Why do you want to know?"

"I'm curious, is all. Was it around this time of year you sailed?"

"No, it was early July. Now wait a minute, who are you and why are you asking all these questions? You take notes all the time! Are you part of the steamship line?" Kate's voice hardened.

"No, no, not at all, I'm just interested. I'm an author and I'm collecting information for my book. I'm sorry to have distressed you. Nothing you say will get back to the steamship company." She didn't mention the 'book' she was writing was an undercover report for the American government immigration department. Ethel Watson faded into the gloom of the cabin, something she seemed adept at.

Brigid Murphy's story terrified Bella. "But … But … What can I do?!"

"Is your family on board?"

"Yes, my Ma and Da and my brother." She thought of George's size and found it comforting.

"Keep as close to them as you can. That'll help. You must understand, though, we women can't help you if he comes in here, we can't chance losing our entry into America. The worst times are just before breakfast and late at night. He, and others, take delight in coming in here when we're dressing or undressing."

Bella nodded in understanding. "I need to talk to my folks right away, I'm supposed to meet them in the dining area but I've no idea how to get there. Can you help me?"

"Of course, it's about half way back in the center of the ship." Brigid changed tack. Is there anything in your bag you don't want to lose?"

The change of subject puzzled Bella. "Yes. Why?"

"Because some of our sisters here have light fingers!' She glared around the assembled women. "Is it something you can take with you?"

"Yes, it's a piece of jewelry from my Gran."

"Bring it along or someone will steal it before you get back." Kate cast her eye over the interested listeners. "Leave the rest of her belongings alone, you understand me?!" There was a mixture of replies, ranging from "Yes, Kate." to muttered oaths under breaths. One woman, Mabel Brown, older and harder than the rest, was about to voice her resentment but a glare from Kate stopped her cold. Mabel was coarse of skin and voice, spiteful, gossipy and world-weary with just enough of her youth left to attract men by her immodest demeanor. She had already found comfort in the arms of the Chief Steerage Steward's second in command, Billy Surtees, during the short voyage north from Liverpool. Mabel made a living filching valuables from the valises of steerage class passengers, men in particular. Kate meant the warning for her. Bella rummaged through her valise, found her Gran's cairngorm brooch and pinned it on her blouse. Kate led Bella through the underground warren of passageways, pointing out the signs which would help Bella find her own way. Harry and Fiona were there already, George hadn't arrived yet. Bella explained what had happened and Kate filled in the details.

The news appalled Harry and Fiona. "How can he get away with this, I'm going to demand to see the Captain!" This was Harry.

George arrived in time and noticed three things, first, Kate was most attractive, second, something had upset his sis and his ma, and third, his father was stotting mad!

"What's this about seeing the Captain?"

They told the tale again, with a similar result except now George joined the throng of the irate. Ever a man of action, he was all for confronting the scum and making him aware of the dire consequences should he harm a hair on Bella's head.

"But what about him having the power to prevent us from landing in America?" Bella was strung tighter than Harry's fiddle.

"Can he do that?" George posed his question to Kate, wanting to hear her voice once again.

"He says he can but I've no knowledge myself."

Harry had been thinking through the dilemma. "Here's what we do. George, you and I will take it in turns to stick to Bella like glue, early in the morning and late at night in particular when this predator is about. Now, we can't go into her cabin but we can stand guard outside her door until the danger times are past."

"Good idea. Bella, spend all your waking hours with us and you'll be fine. Kate, you'd be welcome too!" George beamed his best smile. Men!

#

Bella was safe for the first three days of the passage because everyone in steerage was seasick. There's nothing like a thousand people throwing up to cool a rake's ardor! It happened as soon as the Curambria left the shelter afforded by Ireland and first faced the rollers speeding across the Atlantic. First a hush came over the passengers, then green gills appeared followed by a mad rush to the tiny deck reserved for the steerage class. There wasn't enough room along the rail for all who needed to be sick, and the seamen's calls for passengers to be on the downwind side were unheeded. Before long the deck and its occupants were an aromatic disaster.

Bella wasn't immune to this malady but she kept to her berth, moaning and groaning with each roll of the ship. First, she was afraid she would die, then she was afraid she wasn't, a sentiment shared by all her cabin companions. Her ma managed one visit before she too succumbed. At last, Bella seemed a little better and struggled along to the little dining area, hoping to find her family. No such luck, but she managed a little food for the first time in ages. Lederbeiter, the amorous officer, came in search of her.

"Ah! Miss Gordon! Glad to see you up and about. How are you feeling?"

Just seeing him made Bella feel sick again but she knew the need to be civil. "I'm fine, sir. Have you seen my family?"

"No, Miss Gordon, why don't we go look for them. I have an idea where they might be."

Bella's heart leapt in fear, knowing just what the officer had in mind. Just then, a larger wave than normal hit the ship causing Bella to lurch into the officer's arms, much to his delight. This turned to disgust when Bella's stomach rebelled yet again and she spewed all over his white uniform. The officer pushed her away in revulsion. "You stupid bitch, look what you've done. I'll make you pay! You'll get your comeuppance! You mark my words!" He rushed off to sponge his clothing. Despite her queasiness, Bella relished her victory. *That's one way to keep him at arm's length!* But she had seen into the officer's soul and glimpsed the white-hot anger and contempt he held for women. She returned to her cabin to clean up as best she could in the cold seawater provided.

Kate and the other women laughed with her when she told her tale.

"That'll teach him!"

"Can you be sick for 5 more days, we'll be in America by then?!"

"Oh, I'd love to have seen his face!"

"No, you wouldn't." thought Bella. She shivered at the memory of the spite and hatred she had seen. The worst was yet to come, she felt it in her bones.

Chapter 17

The next five days were a nightmare, each day a war, strategic moves, advances, retreats, new combatants, old enemies. In the morning and in the evening, George and Harry kept vigil outside the single women's quarters, fending off all men who wanted access. Most of these lechers shrugged their shoulders when told this cabin was now off limits and moved on, searching for sport elsewhere. But Lederbeiter was livid. First, he tried to bluster his way in but George, who was the guard, was adamant.

"Nobody gets in while the lassies are changing … sir!"

The additional sarcasm enraged the officer even more but George's size deterred him from pushing his luck. Lederbeiter thought about bluffing George with the "Kicked out of America" threat but figured if George felt there was nothing to lose, he, Lederbeiter, would find himself in a very painful physical confrontation. He retreated to consider new strategies.

Once 'the lassies' were up and about and presentable, Bella kept as close to her family as possible. Many of the single women in her cabin helped too. Led by Kate, they acted as sentries, reporting back to Bella where the scum was at any given time.

There was one benefit to all this cloak and daggery, Harry's turn as watchman gave him a chance to play his fiddle. He'd stand guard in the corridor outside Bella's cabin in the near dark and play from memory, letting his fingers caress the strings as a lover might trace the night-time face of his sweetheart. Soon, his audience was too large for the passageway so, when Bella emerged from the cabin, they moved to the tiny dining area, then to the steerage class deck when the dining room also became overcrowded. Word spread and other musicians appeared, dusting off their instruments, testing, tuning, tightening, joining in with Harry's tune, shy at first until they found their voice. And an eccentric collection of instruments it was! More fiddles, but also accordions, chanters, a violin slumming, mouth organs and harps, even a zither. "My Bonnie Lies over the Ocean" never sounded so strange or so welcome to the immigrants. Bella was at peace here, she was safe, amongst her family and friends, and began to enjoy herself. Her sweet soprano voice led many a chorus so she and her Da became well known and popular with the other passengers, at least those who loved music.

Much to her delight, she met up with the Welsh family from the Stewart Line's underground immigration office. The food on the ship was plain but substantial and it was clear the two starving little 'uns had eaten and eaten. The sparkle was back in their eyes and the mischief in their hearts. Even their ma seemed less defeated. Their Da, as expected from a man from the Welsh Valleys, had a magnificent tenor voice and he accompanied Bella on a couple of tunes. He spoke to Bella after one of those duets. "My wife and I will never forget your kindness. I know it was just a roll you gave the kids but it showed my wife there are still good people in this world. We've had a hard time of it these past twelve months, what with the colliery shutting down and there being no jobs. Gwen had almost given up. But thanks to you, she's feeling at least a little bit better. God bless you!" Bella colored and would have brushed it off as a mere nothing but Evan Morgan left to corral his youngsters.

This aura of safety was an illusion. Lederbeiter aimed to have Bella and if a frontal assault wouldn't work, thanks to Harry and George, then he'd have to come up with subterfuges. Each morning, he met with his staff in his cabin. Although it too was on the steerage deck, the cabin couldn't have been more different than his charges'. While still small, the perks of being an officer ensured it was well appointed. It housed a cozy bed, a desk, an easy chair and a water closet and sink. The furnishings were cream and tan which added to the spacious feeling. There was just the one porthole but the light it brought in magnified the airiness and comfort. Lederbeiter's own personal touches were in good taste, striking even, it was an attractive room. This was in stark contrast with Lederbeiter's own appearance. A man in his forties, fleshy, dissipated, paunchy, he was rumpled and red of face with a skin condition that never seemed to leave him.

"Right, men!" He told his stewards, "I need to get Bella separated from her family. And you'll help me."

His assembled staff responded in different ways. Most of them found the Chief Steerage Steward's behavior to be abhorrent and despised his ongoing abuse of the youngest females in steerage. However, they depended on him for their livelihood so hid their feelings along with their principles. The bolder of them chose passive resistance to assuage their consciences, paying lip service to the Chief's scheming but not doing anything to advance his cause. The minority, however, supported their boss and followed his lead in the pursuit of sexual favors.

"Billy, you've already picked up a woman on this trip, have you not?"

"Yes, sir, I have. Her name's Mabel."

"And isn't she in Bella's cabin?"

"Yes, sir, she is."

"Good. Find out from her when Bella's alone. Anywhere in steerage."

If George and Harry were Lederbeiter's first obstacles, Billy's report the next day was the second.

"I've talked to Mabel, she says Bella's never alone, if she's not with her family she always has a giggle of women from the cabin with her."

Lederbeiter smacked Billy hard in the face for his report but consoled himself knowing the days, and nights, still to come before arriving in America. Ever methodical, he retired to plan his next assault. Bella was safe for another day.

Next day's meeting. "Billy, talk to the other women, let them know they'll never get into America if they don't cooperate."

"They know, Mr. Lederbeiter, but I'll remind them again."

Billy's unsubtle reminder scared off a few of the women but hardened the resolve of Kate and her friends.

Another morning, another new tactic. "Billy, get Mabel to invite Bella to the immigration presentation in the dining area. Just her alone mind! I'll snatch her between her cabin and the dining cabin. Don't tell Mabel why, this women's suffrage nonsense may have infected her."

Billy told Mabel what she was to do. Choosing a time when Kate wasn't around, Mabel invited Bella to the meeting. But the last few days had hardened Bella's innocent nature into a suspicious one. "Why me?" She asked. "Are the rest of the girls invited too?"

Mabel didn't have a ready answer, she wasn't the smartest pig in the pen. Bella understood what was going on at once.

"You're on their side, aren't you?! You're trying to get me into Lederbeiter's bed! How could you?! You heard what Kate said about the wee Irish girl, do you want me on your conscience?" Bella carried on and on, allowing all her fear and frustration to spill out onto Mabel.

Kate came into the cabin in time to hear the end of Bella's harangue. "What's going on?"

Bella told her of Mabel's invitation and her suspicions. Kate agreed with Bella's interpretation and added her own verbal assault on Mabel.

"What a poor excuse for a human being you are, you deserve to get a right thrashing, so you do! Get away back to yon fancy boy of yours and tell him we'll *all* attend the presentation!"

Mabel scuttled away, head down, clutching her shawl about her shoulders, but returned fifteen minutes later sporting a cut lip and the beginnings of a black eye. Billy hadn't been happy with the RSVP. Mabel got no sympathy from the cabin.

There was one day left before the Curambria arrived in New York and Lederbeiter was obsessed with having Bella. At his morning meeting with his staff… "Here's how it's going to be! We need to be smart about cutting Bella out of the herd of bloody women and separate her from her family. So, first, we get them all together in the same place at the same time. After lunch today, we'll hold a music competition on the steerage deck. You two, make sure all those idiots who have been caterwauling out there all week are there, threaten them if you must, you know the drill. Just make sure Harry Gordon and Bella are there, the mother and brother will show up too, that's for sure."

"Boss, how about I ask the Chief Steward for an award for the best performance? A prize'll make sure all the musicians will show."

"Good idea, Billy, the Chief'll have something. Go and ask him." He motioned to one of the other stewards. "Find Charlie Brumbage, the Petty Officer, and tell him to come and see me. Where is he? How the hell should I know, he'll be working wherever sailors work at this time of day! Ask around and find him, you dimwit!" There wasn't much love lost between the sailors and the stewards but Charlie

Brumbage had been Lederbeiter's drinking and whoring companion on many voyages.

Billy came back with the prize, a pewter tankard with SS Curambria etched on the side. Billy didn't say how he acquired it, whether the Chief Steward volunteered it or it had been conscripted. Charlie Brumbrage showed up soon after. Lederbeiter told him what had transpired beforehand, about spying Bella as she boarded the Curambria, how she had got wind of Lederbeiter's intentions and had made it difficult to get at her. Brumbrage's eyes gleamed, he was just as dissolute as Lederbeiter and always interested in getting young attractive female passengers into dark corners.

"So, Charlie, Billy, here is what we'll do…" Lederbeiter laid out his plan to Brumbrage and his steward. They rehearsed and polished and changed and rehearsed again until each knew his part and was confident in his ability to carry out the plan. This would separate Bella from her family and friends if anything would.

Brumbrage had a final question. "Where will you be, Wil?"

"I'll be waiting in her cabin; all the women will be at the concert."

"And what's in it for me?'

"You can have her after I'm done!"

The two men grinned at each other.

Next day, Lederbeiter's plans clicked into place like clockwork. First, Billy made sure all Bella's cabin mates were at the concert, using Bella's performance as the motivation to get them to the steerage deck.

Lederbeiter organized the acts so Harry and Bella's song was near the start of the concert. Harry was accompanying most of the singers and dancers anyway so he'd be on stage almost the whole time. Charlie Brumbrage, the Petty Officer, waited until it was Harry and Bella's turn and immersed in their ballad before approaching Fiona and George. He arrived in his most formal coat and hat and talked to them both with all the authority he could muster. Lederbeiter was watching from an upper deck, gnawing his fingernails in anxiety. If Charlie couldn't persuade the Gordon's, he would lose his last chance to get Bella.

"Mrs. Gordon?" Charlie touched two fingers to his hat. "May I have a word? My name is Chief Petty Officer Reginald Sousa and one of my charges is the passengers' baggage."

He had Fiona's attention, George's too for that matter. "Is there something wrong?"

"I'm afraid so, Ma'am. My men were in the baggage hold this morning getting ready for unloading tomorrow in New York. They found several trunks had sprung open during the storm earlier this week. We're asking all the owners of these trunks to come down now and identify their belongings. It all got mixed up, I fear." Charlie held his breath, *"If they don't buy my patter, Lederbeiter will be thwarted and guess who he'll take it out on."*.

Fiona was all for rushing off but George pointed to Bella. “How about Bella, Ma? Her tune will be over soon.”

Charlie jumped in again. “Oh, she’ll still be here when we get back, she’s got a following now and they’ll take care of her. Come on, you wouldn’t want those other women pawing through your clothes, would you?”

Fiona couldn’t bear the thought of foreign hands rummaging in her trunk. She nodded her agreement to Charlie. “George, it’ll take five minutes at the most, Da will take care of Bella after this set.”

George’s concern for Bella and his need to accompany his mother tore him in half. Fiona couldn’t be left alone with a strange man. If she was to go, he had to go too.

The three left in haste, leaving the watching Lederbeiter in a state of high excitement. His plan was working at last, and he was anticipating what was to happen next.

Charlie led the way to the baggage hold, steering the Gordons along corridors even darker and dingier than the steerage class companionways. After what seemed like ages, Brumbrage stopped in front of a nondescript door, heaved on its handle and opened it. He stepped back to let Fiona and George precede him. George entered first and had trouble seeing where he was in the minimal light. By the time he realized he wasn’t in the baggage hold but in a paint locker, Fiona had followed him and Charlie had slammed the door and dropped the bar in place.

Brumbrage ignored the Gordon's shouts and raced back to the steerage deck. He gave Lederbeiter a nod. Lederbeiter pointed with his chin to where Bella was sitting, waiting for her next gig. Harry was still playing, accompanying a rather good Swedish baritone.

Brumbrage again touched his hat. "Miss Gordon?"

"Yes, I'm Bella Gordon."

"I need your help at once. Your mother's injured and she asked you to bring bandages." Brumbrage didn't elaborate, knowing Bella's imagination would race to the worst possible conclusion.

"Bandages? But what happened? I don't have any bandages. Where's my brother? Where is she? Is she all right?" The questions would have kept tumbling out but Charlie held up his hand to stop the torrent.

"Miss Gordon, I'll answer all your questions on the way to help her, but first we must get the bandages. She suggested you might have a spare petticoat in your cabin we could use?"

Brumbrage took Bella's elbow and steered her towards the cabin. Bella changed from shock to action without too much thought in between.

Lederbeiter, from his vantage point, could see the concern on Bella's face. It was obvious she wanted to wait for Harry to finish too but Charlie was urging her to help her ma right away. As Charlie led Bella through the crowd, Lederbeiter left his post and hurried to get there before them.

Bella would have run but Charlie walked in front of her to give his pal time to arrive first. When they got to the cabin door, Charlie opened it, stepped back to let Bella enter then shoved her hard so she'd be off balance. Bella screamed once before a hand clamped over her mouth and an arm snaked around her waist and swung her round so her back was against the bulkhead.

"Remember me, little one?" Lederbeiter hissed. "You're mine now, I've locked your family in the paint storage and we have all the time in the world. I'm going to enjoy this. I can't say the same for you, though!"

Chapter 18

David was bored out of his mind. Nine days into the ten-day voyage and he was tired of waiting to get to America, he wanted to be there. Now. He wanted to start the search for the mysterious Baron Tookov and find out more about the mine. He had done what he could to glean information about both subjects from his dinner companions and his knowledge of Arkansas mining far outstripped what he had learned about Tookov. He was pleased to find Pinkerton enjoyed a reputation for thoroughness even if there was also an indication they used strong arm tactics at times. *Not a bad thing if we ever catch up to Tookov.* David mused to himself. But here he was, one more day of terminal lassitude to endure before getting to New York. He had exercised with Tam in the gym, was finishing his lunch and the day spread out before him like an empty page. Ah yes, the gym. David smiled. That was likely to be the most memorable moment of the day. How wrong he was.

David had met Tam at 6 AM in the diminutive gym, the crack of dawn perhaps but bearable because traveling west meant an extra hour in bed each day. They were not alone, a small group of young American students on their way back from an international sporting competition in London often preceded them. David and Tam had come to like most of the students, they were fresh, engaging and fun. David had at first been envious of their light-hearted approach to life, but laughed at himself when he realized what he had been thinking. *I'm not a candidate for a bath-chair yet!* It had, however, reminded David of the responsibilities he was bearing.

David and Tam's exercises intrigued the students who gathered round to watch. The stretching was common enough but the thrusts and parries with hands and feet had been foreign to them.

"What are you doing?" One student, a fellow called Ian Kirkpatrick from Princeton, had asked. "Is it useful in real life or is it just for show?"

His question had been serious and Tam, who had learned the techniques during his army posting to Hong Kong, took no offence. "Yes, sir, it's useful when you need to defend yourself and you're unarmed. It's called jujitsu."

There was one student who didn't fall into the 'likable' category. Brian Carmodie was a boxer from Harvard, big, heavy, muscular and shunned by the other students. David had noticed in previous mornings he had a cruel streak in him, beating up his sparring partners who were often well below his weight class. He was also missing the ability to censor his words before he spoke so offended everyone on a regular basis. "Hah! That's a game for sissies! Something like ballet. You can't defend yourself by dancing around. Now take boxing, for example, there's a sport for men. You can defend yourself perfectly well if you box like I do!"

David had seen Tam smiling to himself and had shaken his head at him. "Don't!" David had mouthed. Tam nodded his head in sad agreement.

But Carmodie hadn't left it alone. "No wonder England's losing its empire if jujitsu is being taught. Turning them all into a bunch of fairies!"

Carmodie had now attracted David and Tam's full attention. Calling them 'fairies' had been bad enough, but implying they were 'English' was much worse. Tam had turned to David, pleading with his eyes. David had thought about it for a second, then nodded.

Tam had turned back to Carmodie. "Would you care to test whether boxing or jujitsu is the more effective fighting style?"

"What's this, old man, you want to spar with me?"

"Oh no, sir, I was suggesting full contact, if you're man enough?"

For the first time, Carmodie hesitated. He glanced to his fellow students for guidance. They, sick and tired of having to put up with him for the past month, egged him on.

"Go for it, Brian, he's just an old man!"

"Show him how it's done, Brian, give him a lesson."

Brian had failed to notice the winks passing between the students. Even if Carmodie had prevailed, which seemed the probable result, perhaps Tam would get a few licks in and take Brian down a peg or two.

"Okay, old man, you're on. Shall we say best two out of three rounds, two minutes apiece, or is three rounds too much for you?"

“No, that will be fine.” Neither Tam nor David had thought the contest would last anywhere near that long. “Do you need time to warm up?”

“No, I’m ready, old man!”

Ian Kirkpatrick had hesitated then agreed to be Carmodie’s second, David acted on Tam’s behalf. The students cleared the center of the gym and formed a ring round the sides. One of the students had brought his watch with him and became referee.

“Ding, ding, Round 1!” called the ref.

Carmodie had shot across the ring like a cannonball, hoping to surprise Tam. He had unleashed a roundhouse haymaker which, if it had connected, would have knocked Tam half way back to Ballboyne. Tam had stepped inside the punch, grabbed Carmodie’s arm as it whistled past his ear, turned with the punch and bent over. To his astonishment, Carmodie found himself airborne, somersaulting head over heels and landing hard on his back on the parquet floor.

The students had been silent, then exploded in amazement at what they had just witnessed. Carmodie had the wind knocked out of him and just lay there. The referee was just as awestruck and it had taken him a good twenty seconds to remember his role, “Ding, ding, end of round 1!”

Kirkpatrick had helped Carmodie to his feet, led him back to his corner and splashed water on his face. “You’ll have to fight much smarter!” he whispered in his boxer’s ear. “Keep him at a distance, box him!” Carmodie had nodded and dried off his face.

They were whispering in Tam's corner too. "Don't hurt him, Tam. He doesn't know any better!"

"I suppose you're right, sir. I'll just make sure he gets the point and isn't as arrogant to us 'old folks' in the future."

"Ding, ding, Round 2"

Carmodie had left his corner with much more caution this time, hands held in the classic boxing pose, elbows down and in, hands in front of his face, advancing one shuffling step at a time. Tam had been just as cautious but much looser, arms bent, hands open, dancing on his toes, circling to his left, forcing Brian to move the same way, putting distance between Brian's big left hand and Tam's head. Brian had flicked out a left jab, range finding, Tam had swayed to his left and the bare knuckles grazed his ear. David had noticed Brian pulled his fist back at once, remembering what had happened in the first round. Tam had made no offensive moves, just circled round to his left, waiting for the right moment. Brian had been in no hurry either, jabbing and moving, jabbing and moving. He had worked the 'ring' well, keeping away from Tam. Exploratory jabs from Carmodie, Tam had just circled and circled. At last, Carmodie had become tired of the inaction and had thrown a left/right combination. Tam, as usual, had swayed inside the left but, to Carmodie's complete surprise, grabbed Carmodie's right fist in his open hands and levered it down hard against the wrist. Carmodie had yelped in pain and tried to jerk his hand up, all thought of offense gone. Tam had borne down on the wrist, Carmodie had kept yelping, the students had kept shouting their appreciation, David had grinned. Carmodie had come to his knees with Tam in complete control of him.

David had nudged the referee. "Oh, yes, end of round 2 and of the match. The winner is ..." Hurried consultation with David. "Tam Mackenzie! Two rounds to none!"

The students had crowded round Tam, congratulating him, patting him on the back, asking questions. Carmodie sat on the floor, all alone, massaging his wrist, trying hard to be a good sport but failing. *I'd hate to be the next person in the ring with him.* thought David.

#

David finished his second cup of coffee, contemplated a third but chose to go exploring again. He was familiar with the public rooms and accommodations set aside for the First-Class passengers and his previous explorations had taken him to the Second-Class deck. Today he decided to see what the steerage class passengers enjoyed in the way of lodging.

There was a sailor posted at the top of the companionway which led down to the bowels of the ship, but he was there to guard against the riff-raff from below spoiling the pleasures of the upper-class passengers. When David asked for directions to the steerage deck, the sailor smirked, gave David a knowing wink and told him which companionway to take.

David found himself in a scene from Dante's Inferno. No natural light crept down here, precious little artificial light either. Electricity had been available for years on the liners but there were few lamps here in these dark recesses abutting the steering mechanism. The companionways had metal floors slick with oil and dangerous to descend. Rough hands polished the handrails down to the bare metal so they glinted in the dull light. The corners of the corridors were sticky and filthy with dirt accumulated over the years. The appalling noise from the engine reverberated unchecked due to the lack of carpeting.

David picked his way to the nearest door and opened it to reveal a scene from hell. He had entered a long, low room packed with cots for single immigrant men, 150 in this room, one room of many. The cots stretched from one side of the ship to the other, row upon row, tier upon tier. Most of the men were on deck hoping to get a glimpse of the Promised Land, even though they were still several hundred miles from America, but David could see how overcrowded and unhealthy these quarters were. The gap between the cots was marginal, with minimal space to squeeze through. The cots themselves were piled high with personal belongings, anything not in the baggage hold was here, lying on the passenger's sleeping berth. But David's sense of smell was most grievously assaulted and made him long for the fresh sea air on deck. His nose identified the scent of tobacco smoke, both cigarette and pipe, rancid booze, the lingering odors of home-cooked 'delicacies' and the ship-provided meals. There were also fragrant remembrances of the home anti-seasickness remedies, like raw onions, which clearly hadn't worked hence the remnants of the vomit from the first days of the voyage. All these plus the normal ship smells of oil and coal and smoke combined to make David's eyes water and stomach churn.

He fled, but not before marking the intense dislike and disapproval pointed his way from the men lounging on their beds. His hurried departure got him turned around so he didn't know how to get out of steerage, back to the sanity of the fresh air topsides. He opened another door, another packed scene from hell for non-English speaking singles by the sound of it. More baleful glares, another hasty exit, another door to open. A sailor scuttled away as he approached. This was different, it led to a much smaller room, still dark, perhaps 15 – 20 cots in here.

As he opened the door, a male voice snarled, "Wait your turn, I'm first!"

David's eyes adjusted and he saw the voice belonged to a ship's officer. He was struggling with a young female passenger and had already ripped her blouse down to her waist. But she was giving no quarter. The officer had one hand over her mouth to muffle her screams for help, his other hand was fumbling with her skirt. The lassie was fighting back and bit him. Her attacker whipped his hand away, cursing. As David started forward to remonstrate, she head-butted the officer square on the nose with great force.

"Why, you little…! Nut me, would you, I'll kill you!" The officer raised a fist to beat her senseless.

Suddenly, his arm was in the grip of an iron vice. David had grabbed it and was holding it firm. Taken aback, the officer relaxed his hold on the girl who seized her opportunity and kneed him in the groin with all her strength. The officer screamed in agony and doubled over. David let go and the officer fell to the floor, writhing in pain, not knowing whether to tend to his gushing nose or his privates first.

David turned to the girl. "Miss, are you all right? Miss Gordon!?"

Chapter 19

David's astonishment at seeing Bella here on the ship didn't last long, replaced as it was by compassion and concern for her well-being. "Miss Gordon, can I help you?"

Bella recoiled in fright and retreated further into the room, not recognizing or comprehending the speaker. All she heard was another male voice, another threat. She skirled for help at the top of her voice, a piercing, distressed scream but no relief came from the outside world.

"Miss Gordon, Miss Gordon, it's me, David Rennie!" He started to extend his hand to touch her but thought better of it.

Bella searched for a way to escape but David was blocking one route to the door and the ship's officer, still writhing in pain on the cabin floor, jammed the other exit. She drew another breath to scream again.

"Wait, Miss Gordon! Look! I'm David Rennie from Ballboyne!" David moved to the only porthole in the dark cabin so Bella could see his face.

Bella couldn't say for sure if it was the Aberdeen accent, or David's use of her name again that gave her pause. Perhaps it was "Ballboyne" that penetrated her stark fear, after all, no one else would know that wee flyspeck. No matter, she stopped and eyed the figure under the light.

"It is you, Sir David! But why are you here?!" She put as many rows of cots between them as possible.

"Sheer chance, Miss Gordon, sheer chance. I was exploring the ship, got lost and opened this door trying to find a way out." David saw her terror and surmised she was equating him with the ship's officer. "I'm not here to harm you. Look, let me get this piece of scum out of here. Are your parents onboard too?"

Bella nodded, still too shocked to speak.

"Where are they?"

"My Da's playing his fiddle on the steerage deck. Ma's injured and in the baggage hold waiting for me. George is with her."

"Ah yes, the big fellow. I'll have them found and brought here to help you. Do you have more clothes here?"

"Yes, my valise is over there." She pointed with her chin, holding her tattered blouse in front of her and keeping a still-wary eye on David.

"All right, Miss Gordon, you're safe now, I'll take this outside (*He kicked the Chief Steward*) and stand guard while you change."

When he opened the door to the corridor, a mob of single men met him with murder on their minds. Bella and her family had become favorites at this end of steerage because of Bella's sunny and innocent disposition and her father's fiddle. They had heard Bella's screams but previous threats from the steward's staff had cowed them and they hadn't dared to interfere. The men were about to take revenge on David until they saw him pulling the Chief Steerage Steward out of Bella's cabin by his jacket collar. They relaxed even more when David asked for rope to hogtie him.

"Gentlemen." David directed his comment to the English-speakers. "I need three men to find Miss Gordon's mother, father and brother. Who knows them by sight?" A dozen hands shot up. "All right, you three, Miss Gordon tells me her father is on the steerage deck, her mother and brother are in the baggage hold. Scatter and find them and bring them here!"

A big Swede called Erik Kjaerstad showed up with rope and bound the Steward's wrists to his ankles. David decided the Steward was going nowhere soon. The Steward had seen the hatred on the face of the mob and was babbling and pleading for his life. While David had no intention of turning him over to the mob, he saw no reason to say so to the would-be rapist.

"Right! You boys, how many of you have found a way to get onto the top decks?" The shuffling of feet among the youngsters showed many of them had also been exploring. "I need four of you to go to the second-class deck and find Tam Mackenzie, my colleague. If you can't find him, get a boy your own age to ask a steward to find him. Bring him down here at once! Go!" A baker's dozen of boys shot off, leaving David satisfied they would find Tam.

David addressed the mob again. "Is there a place where we can talk? I want to get to the bottom of this."

The men told him of the dining area amidships.

"Right we'll meet there in a few minutes and you can tell me what's been going on down here. I'll be along as soon as Miss Gordon's parents arrive."

It was Bella's father who arrived first, barreling through the crowd, full of concern and guilt, but stopping short when he saw David. All he'd heard was someone had attacked his daughter and he'd rushed to be with her before finding out the who and the what.

"Sir David! What are you doing here? Was it you who attacked my daughter?" He bunched his fists into hammers and would have killed David but one of the single men stopped him.

"No way, mate, that's what we thought at first," he gestured to the rest of the mob, "but then he dragged this poor excuse of a man out of your daughter's cabin. The toff's the one who saved her and sent for you and your folks."

Harry noticed the steward for the first time, took a step and practiced football on his ribs. David felt like joining him but stopped Harry instead, a dead steward would be hard to hide.

Freed from the paint locker by their rescuers, Bella's ma and brother arrived on the run. Fiona asking where Bella was and hustled into the cabin. George aped Harry's surprise at seeing David, suspicion at his involvement and, in the end, his acceptance David wasn't the wrongdoer. He too divined the steward's role and took the obligatory kick at the supine figure.

Tam was next to show up, escorted by the boys who had found him. "The boys tell me a woman has been assaulted." He scanned the crowd and recognized Harry and Fiona and George. "Miss Gordon from Ballboyne?!" Tam couldn't keep the incredulity out of his voice.

"Yes," said David, "The one and the same!" David told Tam and Bella's father and brother what he had seen, including how Bella had fought back so well.

George puffed up a tad and told the group, listened to by the crowd, he was the one who had given Bella instruction in how to defend herself. Harry, Bella's father, was horrified, then pleased, David was bemused, while Tam eyeballed George, grinned, stuck out his hand and said, "Not bad for a Black Watch laddie!" The two ex-soldiers nodded and shook hands in understanding.

Fiona, Bella's mum, poked her head out of the cabin. "Bella would like to talk to Sir David and her Da."

David told Tam and George to take the steward along to the dining area and keep him safe from the mob, he'd be along soon. He followed Fiona into the room, Bella was on her cot near the porthole. To David's eye she seemed smaller and frailer than when he had first seen her in Ballboyne. Shock had replaced her recent fear and anger and she sat with her arms wrapped round her legs, rocking, rocking.

Harry brushed David aside and knelt by the bed. "Are you all right, my dear? Has any harm come to you?"

David had to strain to hear Bella's voice. "I'm alright, Da, no permanent damage, I'll have aches and pains in the morning I'm sure but nothing serious. I have scratches and bruises on my arms and I'll have a right walnut on my forehead where I butted him, but that's a bruise I'll wear with pride!" A half smile ghosted her lips but vanished at once. Her eyes shifted to David. "I want to thank you, Sir David. If you hadn't come in when you did, it would have been much worse." She shivered, Fiona held her tighter.

"I only wish I had been here earlier, Miss Gordon. I might have prevented the whole assault."

Bella's voice regained a scrap of strength and her spirit peeked through the shock. "I wish you had been here sooner too! That..., that..., that beast has been after me ever since I boarded. He must have decided this being our last day at sea, now was his final chance to have me."

"He's been after you since you came on board? Is there no one in authority you could complain to?"

"He is the authority here, he's the Chief Steward for Steerage Class passengers. And he's one of many who prey on and leer at and watch and proposition us single women morning, noon and night. It's worst when we wash and dress in the morning, men wander through at will, even in here, and many from the upper decks. But its worst at night when one hears screams from a poor unfortunate soul who wasn't able to protect herself." Bella disappeared into her memories with only the ghosts for company.

"And your family wasn't able to protect you." It was a statement, not an accusation but Harry and George dropped their eyes, feeling guilty, Fiona shooting them a furious glare.

Bella sighed. "They did their best but our accommodations are separate, Mum and Dad are sleeping in a large cabin with other married couples, George, my brother is in with the single men but at the back of the ship, well away from here, I'm bunking in with other single women. It's almost as though they had designed the accommodations for the benefit of beasts like him!"

David remembered the wink the sailor had given him at the top of the companionway. He also understood why the men in the large rooms were so hostile.

"All right Miss Gordon, why don't you stay here with your mother and try to compose yourself. Harry! George! We'll talk to the men in the dining area and find out as much as possible about what women have to endure here, then we'll talk to the Captain and get you away from this hell-hole"

"The Captain? But the Chief Steward said anyone who complained wouldn't be allowed to land in…Oh! He was just trying to keep us quiet, wasn't he? Damn him!" Bella got angry again, then relapsed into tears, her mother stroking her hair and whispering in her ear.

Harry and David hurried to the dining area where Tam and George each had a foot on the Chief Steward. The mob of single men was waiting with impatience, conversing amongst themselves. Word had spread and a smattering of women joined the men in the ripe, airless room.

David stood on a table and the crowd quieted.

"Miss Gordon is in good health, no thanks to him." He nodded to the steward. "I want to know as much as possible about this scum and what the women have been enduring. Tell me everything you know." The scum in question was now trying to shrink himself into a crack in the floor, still believing David would have him torn to pieces.

The cries, shouts, curses and laments unleashed by David's request would have put the Tower of Babel to shame. It was obvious he had touched a raw nerve, a nerve suppressed like lava in a volcano by the Chief Steward's threat of not being able to land in America. At last, free from constraint, they could express themselves and did they ever!

"One at a time," David shouted, "One at a time! You sir, in the suit. What can you tell me? You'll be next, sir, I promise you." This mollified an irate farmer from the west of England.

And so, the sordid tale unfolded, stories of rape and assault and oppression and fear. Of a system designed to isolate the single women to make them easy prey for the crew and, David was ashamed to admit, for upper-deck passengers. *I wonder what those men tell their wives before they come down here.* thought David.

Everyone had at last said what needed to be said. David thanked the group as they dispersed, many up to the deck railing to look for America. He turned to Harry, George and Tam. "All right! We're going up to the bridge and see the Captain, I dined with him two nights ago, he seemed a decent sort. I want this," he pointed with his foot, "under lock and key until we get to port. We'll see if we can press charges but because we are still in international waters, it may not be possible. At least I can get him fired." David mulled it over. "It's unlikely there will be any reprisals against Mr. and Mrs. Gordon, and the steward's men won't bother George, but I'd feel better if we can protect Miss Gordon. Tam, do you have any … connections that would provide Miss Gordon with a safe place to sleep tonight? Perhaps your friend Mrs. Hamm could assist?" David smiled, Tam twigged immediately.

"Yes, Mr. Rennie, I believe she will. May I suggest Mr. Gordon and George accompany you and Bella to beard the Captain on his bridge while Mrs. Gordon and I go to talk to Mrs. Hamm? She'll be willing to help, I'm certain."

George untied the steward's feet and the party was about to snake its way up to Bella's cabin when a short, stocky woman with a suit of sensibility caught David's arm and took him aside. David had noticed her at the meeting in the dining area.

"Mr. Rennie, is it?" David had to bend to hear, her voice was so quiet. "I'm Ethel Watson, an Inspector with the United States Immigration Commission. I am traveling incognito to investigate the conditions immigrants must endure. I heard the information you gathered from the group of single men, and what Miss Gordon had to say. I regret her story is by no means unusual. I'd even suggest that, based on three voyages I've made in steerage so far, it's the rule rather than the exception. I'll be making my report after this trip and would like to include this incident. Would that be all right?"

This shocked David, on many fronts. First, knowing Bella Gordon's treatment was common practice saddened him. No-one, rich or poor, man or woman should be subjected to such abuse. But he was uplifted to hear the United States Government was investigating the matter. An officer traveling incognito?! How novel! He couldn't see the stuffy old British government coming up with such an inventive plan. But of more practical importance was whether he should lend his name and authority to this report. He agreed with the report's intentions, but he was after all attempting to keep a low profile.

"How long before you publish your report, Miss Watson?"

"Oh, it'll be several months, you know how it is, I have to pull all the material together and present it in a coherent manner. How long will you be in New York, Mr. Rennie? I'm hoping you'll be able to be a witness before the Commission."

David hesitated a little longer and decided his efforts to beard Tookov would be concluded one way or another by then. "I'm happy to support your crusade, Miss Watson. I have no objection to including the circumstances Miss Gordon endured. But you must get her own approval. I'd imagine she won't want anything made public until she's passed the Immigration procedures and is safe on American soil. As far as appearing before the Immigration Commission, I don't know where I will be in a few months' time. If I am in New York, I'd be pleased to help."

Miss Watson gave David a calling card and snuck back to her cabin.

David caught up with the others at Bella's cabin and they all went on deck, George and Tam dragging the steward by the jacket of his dull white uniform. The bright light dazzled them at first, but never had clean air smelled better. The seaman guarding the top of the companionway saw the Chief Steward of the Nether Regions bound tight and being force-marched by four angry men and attempted to stop them.

"Oy, what are you doing?! You lot can't come up here anyway!"

The Chief Steerage Steward called for help but George cut off his cries by stuffing a handkerchief into his mouth. Tam glanced at George.

"Myself, I'd have dropped him over the side. Och, I'd have been sporting about it, I'd have untied his hands first, it can't be much more than a 150mile swim!" Lederbeiter paled yet another shade.

David leant into the obstructive seaman, "My name is The Honorable Sir David Rennie of Crachan. I'm taking this man to see the Captain, I caught him attempting to rape a passenger. I aim to have him fired, if not imprisoned. If there are any crew members who have been aiding and abetting this practice, I'll see them fired too. 'Abetting' might include a seaman who knows what's going on down below and allows upper deck passengers to participate. On the other hand, a seaman who doesn't get in our way may well have his participation forgotten. Do I make myself clear?"

David could see the seaman's brain-gears whirring. *"Should I support the steward or hold onto my job?"* He looked at the four determined men, Tam, Harry, George and David, and wisely decided to let them pass. Saying "No!' would be foolish and ineffective anyway. If they wanted to come through the gate, he wouldn't be able to stop them.

"Of course, Sir David, let me help you, I'll lead the way to the bridge." The seaman ignored the glare of pure hate thrown his way by Lederbeiter and led David, Mr. and Mrs. Gordon and Bella along the second-class passenger deck with Tam and George frog-marching the Chief Steward close behind. The party split once they arrived at the companionway to the bridge. Tam took Mrs. Gordon to meet with Mrs. Hamm, passing the responsibility of tending to the prisoner to George. They continued with Bella, David and her father to confront the Captain.

Before leaving, Tam whispered to George, just loud enough for the steward to hear, "If he gives you any trouble, do what I suggested, drop him over the side."

George whispered back "Must I? I'd rather take him back down to the steerage deck and turn him loose among the single men."

The steward blanched like he was about to faint, he hadn't seen the wink between the two ex-soldiers.

The seaman led the rest of the party up past the First-Class deck, causing consternation amongst the passengers, and onto the Bridge Deck. He knocked on the bulkhead hatch and, when a seaman opened the hatch, their guide attempted to enter, but David pulled him back. He didn't want the seaman to give the wrong impression. David and his party entered, dragging the steward, the seaman bringing up the rear.

The Captain, one Hugh Hamilton, was half out of his chair in panic, thinking pirates had boarded his command. He relaxed a little when he recognized David, then stiffened again when he spotted his Chief Steward of the Steerage Deck trussed like a chicken and being manhandled. David approached him with outstretched hand, which Hamilton took as a normal courtesy between gentlemen.

"Captain, is there somewhere we can speak in private?"

"Mr. Rennie, what's the meaning of this?! Why …" And he would have spluttered on if David hadn't steered him to the side of the bridge, using the clasped hand to lead him there.

"Captain Hamilton, this officer of yours attempted to rape Miss Gordon."

Captain Hamilton gaped. "But that's preposterous, he's my Chief Steward for the Steerage Deck!" and Captain Hamilton would have kept on blustering but David cut him off.

"I was the one who caught him in the act, Sir! There can be no mistake. And it gets worse…"

Leaving out the presence of Miss Watson, the Immigration Inspector, David told the Captain all he had found out from the single men, the design of the accommodation to isolate the single women, the steady traffic of men, sailors and passengers alike, the assaults, the screams, the lack of protection by the crew, the fear instilled by the Chief Steward so the passengers were afraid to complain. David laid it all out, accusation by accusation, example by example, and by the end, the Captain's bluster had subsided to wide-eyed fear. He was responsible for the conduct of his men and knew there would be a piper to pay.

When David had finished, Captain Hamilton was silent for a long moment. There were no questions to be asked, no clarifications needed, David had laid out the circumstances so well that there could be no room for doubt. He took a turn round the cabin, deep in thought. Then he exhaled. "I am the Captain of this ship. I am responsible for the actions of my staff. Therefore, I will resign at the end of this voyage. And I will ensure Mister Lederbeiter here never works on a transatlantic liner again. Officer!"

"Yes, sir!" The Officer of the Watch, Mungo McLeod, had been trying hard not to be caught eavesdropping.

"Assign two good seamen from your crew to lock Mister Lederbeiter in the brig. Don't use steward staff, I don't trust them. No-one is to talk to him, so post a man outside the brig to ensure his silence until we reach port tomorrow. Tell the Chief Steward to be available to see me in my cabin at a moment's notice."

"The Chief Steward in your cabin at a moment's notice, yessir!" and the Officer of the Watch dragged

Lederbeiter out. The seaman who had escorted David to the bridge also slipped away.

The Captain paused, running his mind over what else he needed to do. He turned to Bella Gordon and her family. “I don’t think my apologies will have any value, but I tender them anyway. I greatly regret the attack by my steward, I am relieved Mr. Rennie was there to prevent the worst.”

Bella gave David a sharp glance when she heard Mr. Rennie and not Sir David, but David gave a slight shake of his head.

Captain Hamilton turned and asked David if there was any additional help he could offer.

“Yes, Captain. Miss Gordon will stay in a cabin on the second-class deck tonight. I need one of your seamen, not a steward, to escort Miss Gordon and myself to steerage and bring her luggage to Cabin 207. You have a Doctor on board?”

“We do, sir.”

“Please ask him to come to Cabin 207 in half an hour.”

Bella protested she was fine but her father cut her off. “If you’re fine, then there’s harm. If you’re not fine, now is the time to find out. Don’t forget, you have a medical examination tomorrow at the Immigration Office.”

Captain Hamilton made sure his staff noted all David’s requests, then said to David, “If there’s nothing else, Mr. Rennie, I’d like to talk to my Chief Steward. Mr. Bogie, my First Officer, will accompany you and make certain you get whatever you desire. Mr. Bogie!"

"Aye, aye, sir!"

"Make sure Mr. Rennie and his party receive the utmost consideration and respect, and they get access to any part of the ship they wish."

"Aye, aye, sir!"

David saw the captain was doing his best to right the wrongs committed on his ship, but it was too little, too late. He led his troop off the bridge.

"What now, Mr. Rennie?" asked the First Officer.

"Let's get Miss Gordon's valise."

Chapter 20

In Arabia, they say its dawn when you can see the difference between a black thread and a white one. That distinction was still a long time coming but already immigrants lined the rails of the steerage deck, eager to see The Promised Land. Those who had stayed on deck all night, and there were many, told newcomers about the flashing light appearing about four in the morning. Ah! A lighthouse! Land! America!

"What's thon lighthouse, then?" asked one excited traveler of an idling deck hand.

"Montauk Point. It's at the east end of Long Island."

"Are we near New York, then?"

"Aye, but you've still got six hours steaming ahead of you."

"6 hours?! Must be a bloody big island, then!"

"Everything's big in America, mate, everything!"

The immigrants couldn't decide between staying where they were and watching their new life unfold, or losing their place on deck by going below and eating a hearty breakfast, not knowing when they would next eat. The upper decks were not so crowded, the first and second-class passengers were better informed by their stewards and recognized there was no rush.

David, however, was up and about. He couldn't sleep. In part, his sleeplessness was because of the tasks looming in front of him in the pursuit of Tookov/Thomas. But it was Bella and her incursion into his life that kept him staring at the ceiling most of the night. Until yesterday, the ocean voyage had been a pleasant interlude, or, perhaps the calm before the storm might be a better way to put it. Now, the steps he needed to take to find Tookov once on terra firma were just as real but Bella's presence distracted him. He felt protective of her, but that was nonsense, he didn't know the lassie. Was there any obligation on him, just because she came from the same village? Would he be having this conversation with himself if she was old and ugly? He paced up and down his cabin, hands behind his back, head on his chest, then stopped in his tracks, checked himself in the mirror and laughed. *My, my, David!* he said to himself. *This isn't what Tam taught you. What was it he used to tell me? 'Separate the necessary from the desirable from the impossible, then act.' Right, now, get on with it.*

An hour later, Tam joined him and found him clear-minded and determined.

"Tam, before we land today, I need to make sure Miss Gordon is all right. I also need to know more about their destination. I'll ask Captain Hamilton for the use of his private dining room for breakfast and I want you to invite the four Gordons and Mrs. Hamm to join us there at eight o'clock. The ship docks about eleven so we'll have plenty of time to eat then prepare for disembarking. Make sure they know it will just be the seven of us so the women need not worry about their appearance." Tam smiled at David's naiveté.

The captain, still trying to appease "Mr. Rennie", had agreed with good grace to David commandeering his dining room and instructed his staff to serve the party as though the King himself were present. The dining room seated eight at a round, heavy glass table supported on ornate iron legs with plush and substantial chairs upholstered in rich cream and Wedgewood blue regency stripes. The wallpaper was a subdued version of the chair fabric, topped by cavetto molding. Pictures of sailing ships at war hung on the walls with brass tags underneath them to identify the battles. The overall atmosphere was one of invitation, comfort and style. Harry and George arrived first, somewhat upset at having to tear themselves away from the rail of the steerage deck but calmed by the better view of Long Island seen from the private dining room, even though it was still just a grey smudge on the horizon. Fiona and Bella, escorted by a seaman, arrived soon after. Both appeared tired and pale, Fiona from worry about her daughter, Bella still recovering from yesterday's assault. Mrs. Hamm entered five minutes late, as was fashionable. The Gordons were uncomfortable in the posh surroundings, gazing in awe at the opulent décor and place settings and lapsed into an uneasy silence. David had reverted to his blithering idiot persona in Bella's presence and the gathering had all the hallmarks of a disaster when Mrs. Hamm, bless her, began to regale the ladies with descriptions of the hats worn by the women in first and second class. Soon, she had Fiona and even Bella laughing and gossiping about what they had seen. Tam and George told war stories and found they had both been in South Africa, although twenty years apart. David watched the conversations unfold and would have sunk further into a black depression but Harry made a casual remark about the changes David had instigated in the forestry practices around Crachan and soon firs, spruce and pine monopolized their discussion.

The waiters, all seven of them, proffered the menus and another opportunity for disaster arose, the menus were in French. Bella saved Harry and Fiona from embarrassment by jumping in and describing each dish. Who would have thought her schooling would first be put to use translating menus off the coast of America!

The atmosphere became even more festive after Tam asked Mrs. Hamm if she wanted more coffee.

"No, thanks," she said. "I'm good."

Tam leaned into her so his eyes were inches from her face and exaggerated his accent. "It's no' yer character I'm interested in, lassie, it's whether you want more coffee!" Laughter all round!

The meal drew to a close and the men lit up their cigars. David tapped his cup to get everyone's attention.

"If I may, ladies and gentlemen …." The table quietened. "First, let me thank you for joining me here today. It's a momentous day for all of us and who knows what the coming hours and days and weeks will bring. I wish us all 'God Speed' and good fortune, and may it be better and safer than the past week." He gave Bella a slight nod, then continued. "I cannot measure the mystical improbability of us all ending up on the same ship at the same time but I'm glad we did. Thanks to Tam's teaching, I'm of the opinion things happen for a reason and we're best served if we choose not to reason why."

Tam saw David was no longer in blithering idiot mode but was in full control of the gathering. He was interrupted, though, by Captain Hamilton himself, abandoning his navigational duties on the bridge to make sure all had gone well.

"Mr. Rennie!" Again, the sharp glance from the Gordons, why was David traveling incognito? "Everything to your satisfaction, I trust?"

"Yes, thank you, Captain Hamilton. The breakfast was excellent."

"I'm glad to hear it, Mr. Rennie. Now, is there anything else I can do to help?"

"Yes, Captain, I'd like to know what happens when we get to New York?"

"Ah, yes. The Curambria will tie up at the Stewart Line pier on the Hudson River. Immigration staff will board and you, Mr. Rennie, your colleague and Mrs. Hamm will undergo a brief inspection. Then you're free to disembark."

"How about the Gordons?"

Captain Hamilton turned to address them. "Because you're immigrating, you will need to go to Ellis Island by ferry for processing. The Immigration Officers inspect your papers. A doctor will check you, it's much the same as you experienced in our offices in Glasgow. The whole process takes four or five hours, though."

"Why so long, Captain?" This was George.

"There are three other ships arriving today, each one is carrying upwards of a thousand immigrants. They have a lot of people to check."

The Gordons fell silent as they tried to comprehend 4000 people. David saw it was overwhelming them.

"It's one last hurdle, Gordons! Then you'll be safe in America!" David turned to address Harry. "I understand you're bound for California?"

"Yes, sire, San Francisco. We plan to catch the train tomorrow."

"And when does the train leave, may I ask?"

Tam looked on in amusement. He had been the one teaching David one caught more bees with honey than vinegar!

"Two in the afternoon, sir, from Grand Central Station. We're traveling on the Union Pacific Railroad."

"One last thing, Harry, where are you staying tonight?"

"We heard we could find a boarding house near the station, I was planning on asking for directions when we get out of Ellis Island." Harry was becoming defensive.

Captain Hamilton interjected. "You must be careful there, Mr. Gordon. Once you leave Ellis Island, hordes of unscrupulous rogues will meet you promising safe passage for you, your family and your baggage. What they promise and what you get may be two totally different things. Their ambition in life is to separate you from your money and your baggage."

The Gordons looked at each other, stricken by the thought of one more difficulty to overcome. The trip had exhausted them, the stress of the emigration in general, then Bella's assault, and, for Harry, the constant decision-making, had worn him down to a nubbin. Life in Ballboyne had been so simple for him, get up in the morning, go to work, come home, play his fiddle. Life-threatening decisions were not something he had experienced, ever. He felt out of his depth and overwhelmed. Even George, the world traveler, appeared frozen in place.

"Perhaps I can be of assistance." David interjected. "Tam and I will be ashore by noon, one o'clock at the latest. Am I correct, Captain Hamilton?"

"Yes. Mr. Rennie, that's right."

"I have business to attend to this afternoon, but Tam here will be at a loose end. It might be helpful if he met you as you leave Ellis Island. He can take you to a small, reputable hotel near the station." David saw the fear of the price to pay at a hotel leap into Harry's eyes. "This will be at my expense. Consider it to be my gift to you for fiddling services rendered!"

David's little joke broke the tension. Harry made a half-hearted attempt to deflect David's offer but, finding no support from Fiona and Bella, he accepted with gratitude.

"Where will we meet Tam?"

"Good question, George. Captain Hamilton, any suggestions?"

The Captain tugged on his beard in thought. "Yes, Mr. Rennie, reuniting families meet at a place on the first floor in the Ellis Island building. Its informal name is the Kissing Post. By the way, the first floor is the ground floor, different from what you're used to in Scotland! Now, if there's nothing else, I have a ship to dock." Captain Hamilton took his leave of the breakfast gathering, wishing them safe travels and a fair wind.

Bella had been quiet throughout the Captain's visit, so it was a surprise when she spoke.

"Will I see you again?"

David had to strain to hear her.

"I was wondering the same thing, Miss Gordon. I feel we have unfinished business here. May I make a suggestion?" No one said no. "If I may impose, perhaps we could meet tomorrow morning at your hotel and I can buy you breakfast. Tam will pick one for you which has a good dining room. Shall we say nine o'clock, then?"

Bella replied before her Da could protest about who paid. "That'll be fine, Sir David. Nine o'clock it is then. And thank you." She dropped a curtsy and led her bewildered family out of the dining room to prepare for disembarking.

Chapter 21

Some cried, some laughed, some cheered, some just stood in awe, their arms around their loved ones. Some were on their knees, fingering their beads and crosses, some were rocking back and forth, wrapped in their prayer shawls, giving thanks perhaps? Giving thanks for the end of the terrible voyage? Or giving thanks for their safe arrival in New York? They were Italian and Irish, Polish and Portuguese, German and Greek, and many more. And there were Scots, including the Gordons. The SS Curambria glided past Lady Liberty, her torch held high, welcoming each and every one of the immigrants. They packed the decks to capacity and beyond, the huddled masses in full evidence, coming to the end of long, many unspeakable, journeys. They had sold everything, wrapped their remaining goods in bundles and walked, sailed, rode or come by train to the ports of Europe. The appalling sea voyage was behind them, America beckoned because Lady Liberty said so. The Gordons were in high spirits, focused on the momentous day ahead. Even Bella had left her blues behind for the moment.

"Look at a' those buildings, Da! They must be 20 floors high!"

Harry could hardly speak, he was so excited. "Bella! Bella! Bella! I'm fair flummoxed! How do you get to the top of one o' them things? It'd take me all day to climb the stairs!"

George was just about to jump in with his theory when James Webb, the Irish lad from the shipping office in Glasgow, appeared at Harry's elbow.

"Mr. Gordon, how are you? How was your trip?"

Harry disliked the young Irishman's familiarity but wanted to talk to someone who had already been to America. "Well enough, thank you. And yours?

"As well as can be expected, thank you, boring, too long. Did I hear you ask about yon skyscrapers?"

"Is that what they're called? Skyscrapers? They're well named. Yes, Mr. Webb, we've never seen them before and wondered how they work."

"Well, I've been in one or two of them myself and they're astonishing craturs! The tallest one is the Park Row building, it's thirty floors high, though I hear there are new ones being built twice as tall!"

"Fancy that! Sixty floors, eh? Amazing, that's what it is, amazing! Tell me, what are they made of? And how do ye get to the top floor?"

"A company called Otis makes and installs things called elevators. They're like boxes on a cable, people go in the box and there are electrical engines pulling the cables up and down. The box stops at any floor you choose." He flapped his hands to demonstrate. "The buildings themselves are a box of steel girders. Oh my, you should see the men building these things, walking along a girder no wider than a plank, a hundred feet and more in the air. Lots of them are Irish!"

Harry shook his head in amazement, it was too much for him to assimilate.

"Well, I must go check on my baggage." said Webb. "I wish you good health and good fortune." He'd been trying to catch Bella's eye but she'd have none of it. Around men, she was numb, petrified, frozen, defenses on alert, with the possible exception of Sir David. Soon, the Irishman was pushing his way through the crowds towards the companionway to the baggage room.

At last, the Curambria tied onto the Stewart Line Pier in the Hudson River. Officials came on board, the Immigration men no doubt, disappeared into the first-class passengers' state rooms, then reappeared, repeated the process with the second-class passengers and left. Bella watched the first-class passengers disembark, searching for David.

"There he is, dear." Fiona, tuned into Bella's emotions as only a mother can, pointed to the foot of the gangplank. Bella tried to catch David's eye by calling his name and waving her handkerchief. She thought she'd been successful because he turned to study the passengers lining the rails of the steerage deck, but realized he was searching for her and not seeing or hearing her amidst the commotion. *At least he looked.* she thought to herself.

Fiona saw the wistful expression. "Don't worry, dearie, you'll see him tomorrow at breakfast."

"Come on, Gordons. Time to pick up our luggage." The family followed Harry down to the hold to claim their baggage and haul it up on deck. Each of them had the biggest trunk the steamship line rules allowed, twenty cubic feet, four feet by two and a half feet by two feet. Like everyone else's trunks, luggage and bundles, they had packed everything from necessities to artifacts to family memorabilia. Harry and George's trunks contained their formal clothes plus spare sets of working attire but also tools they thought might be useful in their new home, wherever that might be. Fiona and Bella had their clothing too but also as much cutlery, place settings, kitchen and cooking gear as they could manage. Small wonder the trunks were so heavy! Harry had made them himself so they were tight and sturdy. The design was basic but Harry had incorporated a few wrinkles of his own. He'd built runners into the bottom of the trunks so they could slide along the floor. He'd also installed rope handles into the ends, long enough to pull the trunks without always knocking their heels. It was still a heavy load but they managed well compared to many poor folk they saw struggling with their bundles and boxes. The Gordons dragged their trunks onto the double-decker ferry and waited for a lifetime for it to fill. About one o'clock, it set sail for the two-mile trip to Ellis Island.

As their feet touched American soil for the first time, a blue-uniformed Immigration Agent tied Inspection Cards onto their clothing and took their papers. The cards had their name, origin, port and date of embarkation and a record of the health checks carried out on the voyage. Bella's card was the same as her family's except for a large "L" scrawled across the front. The agents pushed, pulled and pointed the immigrants towards the imposing Immigration Building and into the Baggage Room, a huge, daunting and confusing space.

"My goodness, Da, what a racket! There must be hundreds of folk in here and they're all talking at once." Bella tried to cover her ears but couldn't block out the sound and haul her trunk at the same time.

"You're right, lassie, but the smell's worse!" The draughts from the open windows couldn't overpower the rancid smell of unwashed clothes and bodies. The Immigration officials once again showed them where to go by pushing and shoving them into place. They had long given up trying to speak in so many languages. The Gordon's left their luggage as directed, with more hope than certainty of ever seeing it again.

Here was the ubiquitous James Webb again. He'd given up on impressing Bella but was enjoying being guide to the Gordon family.

"Be careful as you go up this flight of stairs, it's called the Stairs of Separation. The doctors are at the top watching for infirmities."

The Gordons plus Mr. Webb climbed the stairs with energy in their legs and liveliness in their eyes. When they reached the top, they saw people being taken aside and examined by the doctors. Quite a few of them ended up with a chalk mark etched on the lapels of their clothes.

"What are they doing?" Bella whispered to James.

“The doctors are thinking there’s something wrong with the health of those folk. They won’t get past the counters up there.” he nodded to the front of the room. “Other doctors will give them a more thorough examination. There’s a good chance the inspectors will turn them back.”

“Turn them back?” Bella’s voice rose in fear. “What do you mean “Turn back”?

“Just that, they’ll have to go back to their home country. Watch him.” Again, he pointed with his chin towards a man in his late teens, thin, pale, anxious, furtive, peeking to see what officials might observe him. The doctors had pulled him out of the line, examined him, marked a big E on his coat and waved him forward. Thinking himself unobserved, the man had taken off his coat, turned it inside out and put it on again.

“What’s he doing?”

“He’s hiding the chalk mark but the inspectors up ahead will catch him and it won’t go well for him.”

The Gordons’ anxiety level was already high, Webb had just raised it another notch, the system at Ellis Island was about to crank it up again.

“Here’s where we part, Mrs. Gordon, Miss Gordon. We men go in this direction, you ladies go there. I trust your journeys are safe and sure and America treats you well. Good bye!”

Bella and Fiona clung to each other like insignificant specks of flotsam as the vast tide of humanity swirled by them. They watched in despair as Harry and George left with James Webb.

"We'll meet at thon "Kissing Post" downstairs!" bawled Harry while still in shouting range.

They were in a huge room; far bigger than any room they had ever seen. That would have been the kirk in Ballboyne and this room could swallow ten of them, including the spire.

The Immigration Officers got Bella and Fiona moving again by herding them along like cattle. Now they were in long lines separated by iron railings, inching along towards the final inspection. The émigrés had found it easier to wear their heavy clothes than to take up precious space in the suitcases, trunks or bundles, so were overheated, tired and fractious. Babies squalled, tots cried, older children held tight to their mother's skirts, there were no youths, they had had to become men and women on the voyage. Bewildered, frightened and sullen, the weight and stress of this last hurdle took its toll. The afternoon edged along, three hours, four hours, five hours, old folk collapsing in the hot, humid air. At last, it was Bella and her Mas turn, Bella first. An official took Bella's Inspection Card, saw the penciled L and escorted her to an agent behind a desk, one of many. The agent examined the card, looked Bella over from head to toe and licked his lips. Bella thought he appeared familiar, a family resemblance perhaps?

"Ah, Miss Gordon, I have a report about you from the Curambria. Because of your immoral behavior on the crossing, you will not be allowed to enter the United States, now or ever. People of your low moral character are not welcome as immigrants. The next Stewart Line vessel will take you back to Britain!"

The blood rushed from Bella's arms and legs to the core of her body, ready for fight or flight. Her eyes lost their peripheral vision and focused on the middle button of the official's uniform. Her legs wouldn't support her so she had to grip the front of the officer's desk to keep herself erect. She opened her mouth to shriek but no sound came out. Everything was happening in slow motion, even the official's words seemed distorted.

"Take her to the Detention Pen!"

"At once, Mr. Lederbeiter!"

"Lederbeiter?!" Bella gagged.

"Yes, my dear, Lederbeiter. My cousin has told me all about you. We'll have fun with you yet!" Bella fainted!

Chapter 22

A thousand miles to the south, Baron Pyotr Tookov alias Peter Thomas, knocked his son, Corporal Michael Thomas, to the floor and kicked him hard in the ribs.

"I gave you one thing to do!"

Kick.

"Keep that bloody son of Lord Rennie away from America!"

Kick.

"And you can't even do that right!"

Tookov was screaming now. Michael Thomas curled into a ball, protecting his head and other vital parts of his body.

Kick.

"Get up! Get up, I said!"

The corporal didn't get up, knowing first hand he would be beaten down again. Instead he rolled away from his father and hid amongst the furniture in the best suite in St. Louis' best hotel, The Union Station. Michael's face was a picture of humiliation mixed with pure, white-hot hatred.

Tookov couldn't get a clear kick at his son but continued his harangue. "Why didn't you finish him while you had the chance? Why didn't you try again? And for crying out loud, why did you get a different ship to America? There would have been a dozen opportunities a day to finish him off if you'd been on the same ship!"

The younger Thomas kept silent. He knew from experience his father didn't want logical answers to his emotional outburst, they wouldn't have been heard, anyway. That was his father's way, a very painful way, to be sure, and one he was sick and tired of. How much more of this could he take? It had been like this for years and he'd had enough. He risked a glance at the big satchel visible in the bottom of the wardrobe in his father's bedroom. Once again, he thought the valise held his future.

Thomas the elder kept up his whining. "It was bad enough to have Pinkerton sniffing about, thanks to Lord la-de-da Rennie. I've had to pull out of New York, the city with the easiest marks in the world and now his bloody son is on his way. All because you couldn't handle a simple murder. I'll tell you something, your brother, bless his soul, would have done it no time flat and done it right. Gorblimey, I miss him!"

That was it. Michael couldn't stand to hear how much better his dead brother Jack was one more time. Michael snapped and screamed back. "You great big bag of wind! Whenever things didn't go your way, I get the blame and you hold your sainted son Jack up as the shining star. Huh! If Jack was so bloody smart, how come he's dead, then?! A rival gang jumped him back in London, right?! Jack shouldn't have been on their turf in the first place. Looking for a piece of skirt, wasn't he! Huh! Serve him bloody right. And as for David bloody Rennie, Jack would have done the same as me!"

Michael's outburst astounded Thomas Senior, his son never talked back to him. He lunged for Michael but the younger Thomas put the Baby Grand between him and his father whose anger had now reached homicidal proportions.

The Corporal made his choice, he would get out from under his father's abuse and disappear … with the satchel full of bearer bonds bought with the proceeds of his father's various scams.

The Count gave up chasing Michael and raged around the hotel room, kicking everything he could reach, sometimes to his own detriment. On a good day, he appeared genial, smooth and suave but not today. His volcanic outburst was distorting his face into something out of a Bosch painting of hell. His east-end accent had returned, no more the urbane, knowledgeable international investor, just another swindler feeling the noose tightening.

Then, just as quickly as he had blown up, it was over and he was all business again.

"Listen, I've arranged for thugs in New York to fix David-bloody-Rennie once and for all. We need to get to Rush to fix the mine registration so we own it, not Lord Rennie. I'm sure if we grease enough fat palms we can manage that."

“Why do you want to own a mine? I thought we were going to set up again in Washington and fleece investors as usual?”

“Didn’t you see the American Miners Journal report? It said there’s the possibility of a sizable body of ore and it might be worth millions! That’s why. Why must Rush be such an out-of-the-way place. It’ll take us days to get there. Now, here’s what I want you to do … “

Chapter 23

David and Tam took a coach from the docks to their hotel, the Waldorf Astoria on 5th Avenue in Manhattan. They too were in awe of their surroundings, stretching their necks to catch a glimpse of the tops of the skyscrapers.

"Tam," said David, "It feels like we've come a long way from home!"

Tam agreed. "You're thinking of these buildings, perhaps, Mr. Rennie? You're right. I've seen nothing like them, even in Glasgow."

David relaxed back into his seat and allowed himself the luxury of daydreaming about Bella. *Would he see her again after tomorrow? How had he become so enamored with her? What was the color of her eyes?* At least she was safe now. He sat up a little taller in his seat, proud to have played his part. By the time they arrived at their hotel, David's mind was at ease and he could concentrate on the business of confronting Tookov.

"Tam, I need you to see to the luggage while I deal with our registration. We have a two-bedroom suite booked for two nights under the name of Rennie. Get a member of the hotel staff to sponge my frock coat and top hat right away. I have an appointment at the British Consulate on State Street with Sir Cecil Codlington, the Consulate General."

"What time's your appointment, Mr. Rennie?"

"Three pm, Tam. I'll need you to come with me. I noticed someone followed us from the docks, how many, do you think?"

"I saw three, Mediterranean by the cut of their clothes. Knives, sir."

"Yes, that's what I saw too. Tookov must be getting desperate. He must have something to lose. I'm eager to find out what it is!"

At two-thirty, they caught an open brougham in front of the hotel to the Consulate. David had donned the guise of the British gentleman, top hat gleaming in the afternoon sun, his frock coat with lace bib in place, heavy gold-topped cane between his knees. David had a wave of self-consciousness sweep over him. He almost giggled. *I wonder if I should wave to the crowds like the King does?!* Their three shadows were still there, following them on horseback. Once inside the Consulate, a young man a few years older than David met them.

"David, how are you!"

"Jonathan? It can't be! I'm delighted to see you, but what on earth are you doing here?"

"After our time at school, I went up to Cambridge where, by a miracle I managed double honors. You remember how much I liked to travel?"

David nodded, he recalled Jonathan's wild tales of his foreign travels during the school holidays. His school chums were sure the tales were exaggerated but David knew them to be true. He also knew beneath Jonathan's deprecating exterior beat the heart of a most competent man.

"I squeaked through the Foreign Office entrance exams and here I am, at your service, Sir David!" Jonathan bent at the knee, doffed an invisible hat and bowed in mock ceremony.

Jonathan Moncrieff had been in the same House at Fettes Academy as David so the two knew each other well. A man of many talents, intellectual, athletic and social, Jonathan always dismissed them as being nothing unusual when quite the reverse was true. Above average height, sandy hair with intense green eyes, broad shoulders as befit a rugby player, he would have been of striking appearance except for a bad case of acne. He gave Tam a quizzical look.

David remembered his manners. "Jonathan, I'd like you to meet Tam McKenzie, my friend and mentor. Tam, Jonathan Moncrieff is a school chum of mine." The two men shook hands and "How de do'd!" as appropriate.

"Come this way, gentlemen." Jonathan led them up the magnificent winding staircase to a sumptuous office on the second floor. "Good news and bad news, I'm afraid. Sir Cecil had to go down to Washington to back up the Ambassador on a flap about our concentration camps and such in South Africa. I regret he won't be here to advise you. The Deputy Consulate General, Sir William Wesley, is indisposed with gout, so you're stuck with me, old chap. A glass of sherry, gentlemen?"

The two Scots declined. "Was that the good news or the bad news, Jonathan?" David asked with a smile.

"Both, I suppose. The good news is we have a line on this Tookov fella. He's still in St. Louis, Missouri. He appears to be waiting for someone. He's been asking a lot of questions about mines and registering ownership and such like which seems to fit with what we gleaned from your father's cable. But I'm still shy on the particulars, care to fill me in?"

"Yes, of course, but how did you get this information, Jonathan?

"I'm good friends with the chappie over at Pinkerton, Mike Brown. They do the work and he keeps me informed. Simple, don't you know! Now, how about the details."

David spent an hour filling in the blanks in Jonathan's knowledge. Jonathan had seen the Pinkerton report and asked several clarifying questions.

Once David had finished, Jonathan stood up and lit a cheroot. "It's as I feared. Tookov is operating in a gray area of the law. He's been active in New York; the Police Department have received many complaints from bilked New Yorkers. Tookov left before they could brace him but even if he hadn't, it would have been hard to prove a felony occurred. We know what he did was wrong but there's simply no law on the books to deal with this sort of thing. If rich and greedy people want to invest in something without doing their research, it's their problem. Oh! Sorry, David."

David ignored the implied slight, privately agreeing with Jonathan. "What can we do, Jonathan?"

"The key is he's asking questions about registering ownership. Perhaps the mine has value and he's trying to claim it for himself. If I were you, I'd hightail it down to Arkansas and confirm your claim to it before he does. As far as what to do about Tookov, please, please, please don't take matters into your own hands! Arkansas is a rough place but there is justice of a kind there. I don't want to have to go down there and bail you out of clink! Now is there anything else?"

"Yes, one other matter." David launched into a concise description of what the Gordons and particularly Bella had endured on their transatlantic voyage. "What they endured is disgraceful and must be stopped. I'd like your advice on how to accomplish that."

Jonathan gave the question due consideration. "I've heard rumors about abuse on the ships but no hard facts. Would Miss Gordon talk to me about her experience? I'd also like to talk to this US Immigration Inspector who was traveling incognito. What was her name? Ethel Watson? You say you have the means to get in touch with her?"

David passed Miss Watson's calling card to Jonathan who copied down the information and handed it back. "I don't know the Gordons' timetable but Tam here is meeting them this afternoon to help them settle into a hotel. He can bring me up-to-date when he gets back and hopefully we can find time for you to talk to Bella."

"David, I suggest I write up a formal complaint for you to sign. I'll make sure it reaches the appropriate people in the US Government. I'll also have a word with Miss Watson and see how His Majesty's Government can support her crusade. Now is there anything else? No? Then may I presume on you both to have dinner with me tonight at my club. It's called the Knickerbocker. Is eight o'clock suitable?"

David appreciated Jonathan's courtesy at including Tam in his invitation but couldn't see how Tam could get back to Ellis Island, settle the Gordons, return to the Waldorf-Astoria and change into formal dinner dress in time. Tam saved David the embarrassment of pointing this out to Jonathan. "I'll not be able to do what I must in time to accept your kind invitation, sir. Please excuse me."

Only David noticed the momentary relief flit over Jonathan's face. "You're sure? Must is must, I suppose. Another time?"

"Thank you, sir."

"Time for my appointment with Pinkerton. Their offices are not too far from here, are they, Jonathan?"

"No, just around the corner. Walking distance really."

"Good, we'll walk then." Tam was about to protest but David cut him short. "Thank you, Jonathan, I look forward to seeing you tonight."

As David and Tam left the Consulate, David explained why he wanted to walk. "Firstly Tam, I need the exercise. And secondly, I want to find out from our followers what their instructions are. Here's what I propose …" Tam added his tuppence worth and the pair strode off towards Pinkerton's offices, trying to appear nonchalant but all senses were on the alert.

"Right Tam, three on foot about twenty yards behind us!"

"Agreed, Mr. Rennie, how about the alley on the left?"

"Perfect! Ready? Go!" The two sprinted for the alleyway. David heard shouts behind him as the pursuers gave chase. As soon as David rounded into the alleyway, he skidded to a stop and pressed himself against the wall closest to the followers. The first pursuer to appear was slim, young and short, wearing a black tweed jacket and a fisherman's hat. His hat didn't protect him from the mighty wallop David gave him with the heavy gold knob on the end of his cane and he collapsed like a felled tree, out of the fight. The other two ruffians were older, wiser and warier. They peered cautiously into the alley, then, seeing David and Tam were now ten yards from its mouth, crept businesslike towards them.

Tam was right, they had knives and were competent with them. No overhand stabs for them with the likelihood of a blade bouncing of a rib. No, they held the knives pointing flat towards Tam and David, the blades weaving from side to side. The men were crouched and light on their feet, circling to seize any advantage available. But Tam and David stuck to their position, backs to the wall of the building so they would only have 180 degrees to defend. David held his cane like a bayonet and was effective in keeping his opponent, a tall, dark-complected man with a hook nose and an attempt at a goatee, at a distance. Tam had seen his opponent, medium height, an earring in his left ear, heavy but still nimble was right-handed and had whipped off his coat, wrapped it round his left arm and was using it to parry the knife thrusts. These were the opening gambits, searching out one's opponent's strengths, weaknesses and tactics, thrusting and parrying, finding a soft spot, then attacking.

David noticed his opponent drew his arm back an inch before thrusting the stiletto at him which gave David a slim forewarning. He turned his cane into a cudgel again and, when his attacker showed his intention to strike, David didn't wait for the arm to come forward, but smashed his 'cudgel' down to where he expected the blade to be next second. The weight of the gold top met the assailant's wrist. David heard the bones crack and the knife clatter to the ground. The attacker yelled in pain, doubled over his wrist, holding it to his chest with his left hand and would have run but David tripped him causing him to scream in agony again as he fell on his injured limb. David put his considerable weight on the thug's neck and searched for Tam. He had been so focused on his fight he had neither seen nor heard anything of what was going on beside him. He turned and there was Tam, standing to the side, his assailant also incapacitated.

"What took you so long?!"

David grinned, not surprised Tam had already dealt with his man. "I forgot to warm up, Tam!"

They laughed at each other, the nervous energy now released.

"Let's see what we can find out."

That proved an impossible task, as neither captive spoke English nor any of the languages David and Tam had between them. Tam took their knives, ditched them in a storm drain and let their attackers go, dragging the young thug between them.

At the Pinkerton office, Tam took his leave to return to Ellis Island once he had confirmed Pinkerton would supply four bodyguards for David for the rest of their stay in New York.

Chapter 24

Harry and George were at the far end of the line of inspectors and had no inkling of the disaster that had befallen Bella. Their interaction with the Inspectors was brief but businesslike. The Inspectors examined the sheet the Gordons had filled out in the Stewart Line office in Glasgow (the one asking whether they were bigamists, anarchists or felons) and confirmed the Gordons still gave the same answers. They also checked their destination and the tickets for getting there.

"You have a trade?"

"Yes, sir, I'm a cooper."

"How much money do you have in your possession?"

"Twenty pounds, sir."

"Good, almost 100 dollars, you won't become a burden on the state then, will you?

"No, sir." Harry didn't really understand the question but felt he couldn't go wrong by agreeing with the Inspector.

"Good. Welcome to the United States, Mr. Gordon, and good luck. Next!"

Harry and George descended another set of stairs to the "Kissing Post" and found Tam was there to meet them. They shook hands, the Gordons grinning with relief and pleased to see a familiar face.

"Where are the lassies?" Tam was all business.

"We got separated into two lines, men and women. They should be along any moment now." Harry was searching the stairs for his wife and daughter. But as time passed and the group of men ran out of things to say, they became anxious at the women's non-appearance.

At last, they saw Fiona flying down the stairs as fast as her long skirt would allow.

"What's the matter, my dear, is something wrong?"

"Oh, it's Bella, Da! She got turned back!"

"What!"

"What does 'turned back' mean?"

"Where is she?"

Tam took control. "All right folks, one at a time. Mrs. Gordon, take a deep breath and please tell us what happened."

Fiona gulped a lungful of air, swallowed hard and composed herself a little. "We were waiting to see the Inspector, Bella went first, I waited for the next one. Bella's Inspector was called Lederbeiter and he turned her back!" The men were stunned.

"Lederbeiter?! How could that be? The steward?"

"No, he must be a relative. He said she was immoral and unfit to enter the country!" Fiona was in tears.

"What's this about being 'immoral'? My lassie's nothing of the kind!"

Fiona gulped again. "The Inspector said it was because of her immoral behavior on the crossing. She wasn't immoral, it was the other Lederbeiter!"

Tam took charge. "What happened next?"

Fiona cried even more. "She fainted!"

The men groaned in unison, overwhelmed by their helplessness. They were men of action and wanted to do something, like beat the Lederbeiters to a pulp, but couldn't see a way out.

Tam again. "Then what happened?"

"Two nurses came and took her away in one of those bath chair things. I tried to get to her but they held me back. I was screaming at her but she was still unconscious last I saw her. Then it was my turn and I tried to get my Inspector to understand what had happened, the Lederbeiters and all, but he wouldn't listen. In the end, he told me if I didn't calm down, he'd send me back too. I didn't know what to do." She turned to Tam. "Could Sir David help?"

"I'm sure he'll do his best, Mrs. Gordon. In the meantime, let me see what I can find out. Wait here, please." He left to search for an immigration officer. George started after him but Harry stopped him. "We need cooler heads here, laddie. Let's see what Tam can do."

Tam found an officer and climbed the chain of command until he found an inspector, Charlie Butler, with the authority to match his responsibility. Tam told him the whole story, the actions of the Chief Steward, the attempted rape, Sir David rescuing her, the Immigration Officer, also called Lederbeiter, turning her back for "immoral conduct". At first, Butler was unhelpful, citing rules and regulations, but when Tam told him the name of the inspector who had turned Bella back, his interest perked up.

"Ah, Lederbeiter, eh? Up to his usual tricks, I see. That's different. I'll investigate for you but it won't be until tomorrow morning. I've still got a thousand immigrants to process."

"What will happen to Miss Gordon in the meantime, can't you at least let her family see her?"

The officer's eyes tightened and voice hardened. "Now see here, I promised I would consider it and I will. Miss Gordon will spend the night in the Detention Pen and if what you claim is true, I'll release her tomorrow. One night in detention won't kill her. Come back tomorrow at ten and I'll tell you what I've found."

Tam knew better than to push his luck and left to seek out the Gordons. They cheered up at the thought of reuniting with Bella tomorrow but depressed by her having to stay in detention overnight. They questioned Tam about the minutest detail until Tam tired of having to say, "I don't know." At last he added, "If we get back here at ten tomorrow morning, we'll know more. Mr. Gordon, Mrs. Gordon, we've done everything we can here, let's get you into your hotel and I'll report back to Sir David."

Tam helped the Gordon's find their luggage, intact except for Bella's which had already gone to the detention pen. They dragged the trunks down to the dock and took a ferry back to Manhattan. Tam checked the family into the Albion, a modest hotel the Waldorf Astoria staff had directed him to.

"Right, Mr. Gordon. I suggest you and your family settle into your rooms then have dinner in the dining room here. Please don't concern yourself with the expense, Sir David insists on taking care of the bill. Under the circumstances, it would be better for us to meet here at eight for breakfast, in case we need the extra time."

Harry took Tam aside. "I was thinking the same thing, Mr. McKenzie. We must be packed and ready to leave for California and we don't have time to come back here for the trunks. Our train leaves at two in the afternoon and we can't change the tickets. Fiona and George and me will have to be on the train, with or without Bella! Fiona hasn't worked this out yet and I'm dreading telling her! Help us, sir!"

Chapter 25

David and Jonathan were relaxing with a pre-dinner whisky at the Knickerbocker Club's fine bar. The high lofted ceiling, the wood-paneled walls, the hushed ambience reminded David of his father's club in London. Jonathan was regaling David with details of his trips to the Rockies and California, "… so then the bloody raft overturned and we ended up in the drink!" Their laughter brought frowns from nearby members, just as stuffy as their peers in England.

A porter materialized beside Jonathan. "Mr. Moncrieff, there's a … gentleman downstairs demanding to see your guest. He is most insistent."

"Who is it, William?"

"His name is Tam McKenzie, sir."

"Ah yes, bring him up, William."

"Begging your pardon, sir, I can't, he's not dressed, sorry sir." William didn't like to refuse the request of a member.

"Not dressed? What do you mean he's not …? Oh, not dressed for dinner, is that it?"

"Correct, sir." William agreed, glad his problem, now understood, was someone else's responsibility. "May I suggest the Library, sir? Would that suit? The rules are less restrictive there."

"Fine, bring Mr. McKenzie to the Library, oh, and have three large whiskies brought there too. I fear we'll need them."

"Scotch, sir?"

"Of course, William, of course. Despite what your Kentucky friends might protest, there still is only one real whisky!"

William scurried off to find Tam, David followed Jonathan up another flight of stairs to the Library and took a seat in comfortable easy chairs circling a leather-topped table.

"Tam!" said David. "Come. Join us."

"Thank you, sir." Tam nodded in Jonathan's direction. "Mr. Moncrieff."

"Mr. McKenzie. How are you?"

"I'm fine sir, but I have bad news for Sir David."

"Bad news, Tam? Is it to do with the Gordons? If so, you can tell both of us, Mr. Moncrieff will need to know soon enough."

"Right, sir. Well, it's like this." Tam hesitated, most unlike him. "It's Bella, sir. They turned her back!"

"Turned back? What does 'turned back' mean? Turned back?" David felt a rush of fear turn his face white.

"It appears, sir, our friend Lederbeiter is related to an immigration inspector. He must have got word to the inspector who set it up so Bella would appear in front of him. The inspector declared her immoral and unfit to enter the country and turned her back. Bella fainted, when Fiona last saw her she was being wheeled out in a bath chair."

David was apoplectic by now, searching for someone to strangle with the Lederbeiters at the top of his list. He jumped to his feet and started pacing. He turned to Jonathan. "What does that mean, Jonathan?"

"What Tam said, I'm afraid. The inspectors have the power to turn back certain categories of immigrant. Immorality is one category, madness, poverty, criminals, all are reasons for turning someone back. They will send your Bella back to Britain on the next Stewart line ship, unless we can intercede."

Before David could erupt in anger, Tam interjected. "There's more sir, and it's better news. I found a man in authority over the inspectors, a Mr. Butler, who wasn't interested in helping until I mentioned Inspector Lederbeiter's name. This Lederbeiter has a shady reputation. Butler said he'd consider Bella's situation but couldn't until tomorrow morning. He said if everything I had told him was true, he would discharge Bella tomorrow. I'm to meet him again tomorrow morning at ten."

David relaxed a little. "So where will they hold her? Jonathan, any ideas?"

"Yes, assuming Bella recovered from her fainting spell, she'll be in a detention pen where they keep people who are to go back or are under investigation. They can hold them for a long time. It's by no means comfortable but it is safe."

David was pacing by now. "So, is there anything we can do tonight?"

Tam shook his head. "Nothing until tomorrow morning, Sir David, when we meet Butler at ten."

Jonathan had a far-off gaze in his eye but shook himself and came back to the present. "David, let me give you a little background. Ellis Island and its predecessor, Battery Park, have long had a reputation for corruption. It's been endemic through the Immigration Service but a new broom at the top, a William Williams, is sweeping it clean. A handful of inspectors are in their sights and being watched like hawks. I fear Bella may be the latest in a long string of young, good-looking female victims."

"What do you mean, Jonathan?"

"The stewards select the girls when they're on the ship. They scare the girls, they're vulnerable and easy prey. The stewards have their way with them. When the ship arrives in New York, they arrange for them to appear before one of the suspect inspectors, like your Lederbeiter, who detains the girls for the inspector's enjoyment."

"What happens next?" David felt the cold grip of fear for Bella grab his guts.

"My contact isn't sure. The record-keeping is so messed up it's impossible to trace the girls and they seem to disappear, whether back to their family or somewhere else."

David was far from calmed by his friend's report. "We must find her!" He told Jonathan and Tam about his conversation with Harry and Harry's inability to change the family's train tickets to a later date.

"Sir David, if I may …?"

"Yes, Tam. What is it?"

"The key seems to be our meeting with Inspector Butler at ten on Ellis Island. I suggest we go to the Albion, bring the Gordons up to date while we have breakfast and then find out what Butler has to say. There are too many unknowns at the moment for us to devise a strategy."

Jonathan considered Tam with renewed appreciation. "Well said, Mr. McKenzie! David, your thoughts?"

"As usual, I agree with Tam." David gave a nod of appreciation to his friend. He paused. "Although I think we should keep the worst of the news about the Lederbeiters to ourselves for the time being. No need to tell them about the girls disappearing. Are we clear? Very well, let's go! I suggest we take two carriages, we need room for the bodyguards too."

Jonathan, however, asked to take his leave of the two Scots. "I have connections I'd like to talk to. I may have more information before tomorrow morning. You're meeting the Gordons in their hotel at nine, aren't you?"

Tam spoke up again. "I took the liberty of suggesting we meet at eight, seeing as how there is work before us."

"Good work, Tam. May I join you? I'll have more news for you by then. I'm afraid you'll have to miss a good dinner though; the Knick has a well-deserved reputation for an excellent kitchen."

David understood, without Jonathan as their patron, Tam and himself were no longer welcome.

"We understand, Jonathan. Let's not stand in your way. I pray you find good news." The three sped downstairs, shook hands on the sidewalk and parted. Four large gentlemen surrounded David, courtesy of the Pinkerton agency.

"Tam, how do I get to Ellis Island from here?"

Tam almost said, "Now, at this time of night?" but one glance at David saw him focused, grim and determined to get to Bella. He turned and asked the same question to the Pinkerton men who shook their heads. "The ferry stopped running at eight o'clock, sir."

Tam probed more. "If it was your daughter on Ellis Island, how would you get there?" Again, three of the men shook their heads but the fourth cleared his throat.

"I have a brother who is a fisherman and runs his own boat. If it's worth his while, he'll take you there. He's in need of money."

David leapt at the chance. "What's your name, sir?"

"Ronaldo, sir."

"Good, Ronaldo, take us to him, we need to get there as soon as we can."

Tam opened his mouth to suggest at least a change out of evening clothes, but another glimpse of David's clamped-shut jaw and single-minded gaze kept him quiet.

The six crammed into another coach and sped off to the waterfront. Ronaldo's fisherman brother, Guido, was a small, energetic man boasting a loud voice, black hair with ringlets which would have made any mother proud, (of her daughter), and an eagerness to please for money. David thought he would have done anything to put cash in his pocket…anything. He was glad to have Tam and the Pinkerton men beside him.

Ronaldo rattled off a string of phrases in a dialect which David understood to be an Italian patois. David caught the gist of it and heard the words for money, Ellis Island, nobility, (himself, he presumed) and, again, money. Guido's initial reaction and body language were negative. He took a quick step back, folded his arms and shook his head till his curls swung. Ronaldo spoke again, leaning into the smaller man, gesticulating to the watching group. David heard polizia and money again. Guido unbent a fraction. Then Ronaldo fired his broadside. More conversation with his hands, much gesturing towards the boat, and more mentions of money, accompanied by rubbing his thumb over his first two fingers.

"What's going on, Mr. Rennie? Would you like me to step in?"

David turned away from the brothers and whispered to Tam. "No, Tam, it seems we've reached an agreement." David was almost grinning at the interplay but pulled himself together, this was no time to lose focus.

"Right, let's get going. Ronaldo, come with us, I'll need you to interpret. You other Pinkerton men can go home, I have no further need of you tonight."

The Pinkerton men complained their boss would string them up if they left their duties, which was keeping David out of harm, but David was adamant. He didn't want Ellis Island to think they were being invaded.

Guido untied his boat from the dock, shoved off and hoisted the jib. The winds were light and the tide was in their favor so they took but thirty minutes to cross the Hudson River to the wharf on Ellis Island. Ronaldo gave a quarter of the promised money to Guido to guarantee he stayed there. Ronaldo remained on the boat as further insurance.

"Right, Tam, let's get cracking!" The two Scots marched up to the guardhouse at the front door and woke the night watchman, an ex-navy man with one arm and a crutch. It smelled like he had a bottle of rum to keep him company tonight, maybe most nights. The old man fair goggled at his two callers, one in full evening dress yet, both of whom stank to high heaven of fish. He'd had this sinecure for six years now and these were the first late night visitors to grace his little office so there was fear to go with his overwhelming curiosity.

"Bloody hell, you scared me half to death. Who the hell are you and what do you want?" The watchman took a swig from his bottle to get him over the shock.

"I am Sir David Rennie of Crachan and I need to see your commanding officer immediately." David was too worried about Bella to employ his normal approach which would have included a large dose of charm.

"Well, you can't. Goodbye." The watchman turned back to examine how much courage remained in his pint.

David was about to lean into the little shed and yank the watchman through the window by the collar of his grimy dark blue uniform jacket. Tam interrupted him. "Permit me, sir."

David took a deep breath and stepped back, promising himself he would beat the old seaman to death with his own crutch if Tam wasn't successful.

"I apologize for my impetuous friend here. May I ask your name, sir?"

Perhaps it was the 'Sir' that did it. "Jake Reid, Chief Petty Officer Jake Reid. Who's asking?"

"I'm Sergeant Tam McKenzie and my colleague here is Sir David Rennie. Sir David, perhaps you'd like to take the air for a moment?" Here was one of those commands couched as a question. David took the 'hint' and walked away.

The two old soldiers regarded each other, liked what they saw and nodded. Tam continued. “Sir David has urgent business inside and needs to see an official as quickly as possible. Can you help us?”

“The island is closed for the night, so, no, I can’t help you.”

“There must be someone you rouse in an emergency. Who is that?”

“Captain Brian Clegg is the senior officer on site, but, as I said, the island is closed.”

“You know, Jake, we’d be very grateful, and I mean, *very* grateful, if you could help us. You just need to let Captain Clegg know there is a gentleman wanting to see him. Even if he doesn’t agree, our gratitude to you would still be in your pocket. And Captain Clegg would benefit too.”

The wheels turned and Jake came to the inevitable conclusion. “All right then, but Sir David had better be very grateful indeed!”

Tam mentioned a figure and Jake whistled. “Why didn’t you say so! Come with me!”

Jake unlocked the front door and ushered David and Tam into the massive front hall. He limped through the baggage room to private doors on the far side and rapped on the second door. No response. He knocked again with more force, still no response. He had to open the door and shout to rouse the room’s occupant. Once the heavy sleeper was awake, David presumed it was Captain Clegg, Jake entered and closed the door behind him but David could still hear him soothing the ill-tempered officer. Clegg's tone changed from anger and irritation to interest and avarice, Jake had got around to the 'gratitude' part.

The door opened and a stout gentleman of about fifty appeared, trying to tuck his white shirt into his trousers, button up his fly and comb his sparse, stringy grey hair, all at once. But the sense of comic relief disappeared when he opened his mouth. His strong, deep voice spoke of authority and, despite the promise of 'gratitude', he was wary and still put out by being awoken in the middle of the night.

David had recovered his wits and reverted to his normal 'catching flies with honey' mode. "Captain Clegg, I apologize for my intrusion at this time of night, may I have a word with you in private?"

Clegg was wide awake now. "Yes, come into my office. This had better be good, waking me up at …" he consulted his timepiece "11:30." he grumbled. Tam and the watchman waited outside while David followed Clegg into a small, overcrowded office. It reminded David of the solicitor's office in Glasgow, stacked to high heaven with papers and boxes and files.

David told the story of Bella one more time, the attempted rape by one Lederbeiter, the refusal by the other Lederbeiter to let Bella into the country. He also told of Tam's conversation with and interest shown by his own Inspector, Charles Butler.

Clegg was all ears now. "What would you like me to do, Mr. Rennie?"

"I want you to find Miss Gordon and let me talk to her. I need to see her with my own eyes and that she's safe and sound. I understand she'll have to follow the normal process to get off Ellis Island but I have faith you will find her story believable. By the way, I hope this will help compensate you for your troubles." David slipped a wad of dollar bills into Clegg's now outstretched hand.

"I understand, this is very irregular …" another wad of notes changed hands "but I'll see what I can find out. I'll need to get help to find Miss Gordon." He opened the office door and told Jake the watchman to scare up a Fred Black, a records clerk who lived on-site. The clerk arrived at a run five minutes later, a young man in his twenties, woken from a deep sleep, his fair hair in disarray, his boots untied, nervousness writ large on his otherwise unlined face.

"Captain Clegg, sir, I came as quickly as I could." His words came out in a squeak.

"Never mind. I need you to find the paperwork on a Miss …" He turned to David who finished his sentence. "Bella Gordon, Mr. Black, Bella Gordon."

Clegg continued, "She was on the Curambria, processed today and turned back at Inspection. Bring everything you find as soon as possible!"

David could see the turmoil on the clerk's face. "Where to look? Where to look?" Fred decided on his course of action, squared his shoulders, faced Clegg eye-to-eye, said "Yes, sir!" turned on his heel and ran out the door.

David could see this would be a long search so made his apologies to Clegg, left his office, found Tam and together, they paced the long, dark corridor. At night, Ellis Island was more like a prison than ever. Even though it was only four years old, it had an institutional smell, stale air, stale food and stale people. Despite the hour, it was seldom quiet. The background noise was a cacophony of women crying and men snoring, but shattered on a regular basis by loud, heart-wrenching screams. But worst were the silences that followed. David peeked at Tam, perhaps the most level-headed person he'd ever met, and could see Tam was being affected too.

An hour passed, then David heard the scurrying footsteps of Fred Black returning. Tam and he quickened their pace and arrived at Clegg's office at the same time as the clerk. Fred knocked on his employer's office door and entered on Clegg's invitation.

"What did you find?" Clegg wasted no time in complaining about how long it had taken.

"I have everything you need, sir. Here's the Inspection Card, here's the copy of the Ship's Manifest and here's the records created here."

Clegg glanced at the Inspection Card and Ship's Manifest then passed them on to David. David checked the name, yes, Bella Mairi Gordon. Address, yes, 3 Bridge Street, Ballboyne. Date of birth, mmmh, she is only 17, Tam was right. "Yes, Captain Clegg, this appears to be her right enough. When can I see her?"

“Well, Mr. Rennie, this very irregular.” Clegg inspected the Ellis Island papers a second time, then a third. At last, he met David’s eyes, confusion and more than a trace of fear on his face. “I’m afraid you can’t, Sir David.” he said.

“What do you mean, I can’t?” David’s voice was thundering through the corridors by now, his patience at an end.

“The Inspectors have already shipped Miss Gordon back to Britain!”

Chapter 26

David jumped from his chair but Tam was quick on his feet and stepped between David and Captain Clegg which may have saved Clegg a few teeth and prevented a crooked nose. Tam grabbed David's lapels, pulled him round so they were face to face, stared David straight in the eye and said "Get a hold of yourself, Sir David, don't shoot the messenger. Captain Clegg has done what you asked, found out about Bella. The fact you don't like what he found out doesn't shift the blame to him." Tam's voice was quieter now, as though he was soothing a raw colt, which he was in a way. "We need to find out what this means before we take an action which may well be inappropriate, like murdering a Captain of the US Navy." There was a slight smile on Tam's face now, and a similar slight teasing inflection in his voice.

David had been struggling to get free but Tam's calming words and voice brought a measure of sense back to him and he dropped his eyes, stopped resisting and lowered his voice. "You're right, Tam. Captain Clegg, I apologize, please forgive me."

Clegg accepted the apology and took his hand out of his desk drawer where he kept his pistol. "Apology accepted, Sir David, apology accepted. What else do you need?"

"May I inspect the records created here on Ellis Island?"

"Yes, here they are." And Captain Clegg passed the rest of the paperwork brought by the young clerk.

David brought them closer to the light fixture and examined them. "Hmm, as I feared, our friend Lederbeiter the Inspector created these papers. He had a hand in Bella being refused entrance to the United States and in shipping her back in a hurry. Is it normal to return rejected immigrants to their home countries right away?"

"No, Sir David, it isn't. We hold the disallowed passengers at least overnight, often longer, and their case is reviewed by a special board to confirm the decision made about them. It's very suspicious to have Bella sent back on the same ship she arrived on, and on the same day too." Captain Clegg's mind reviewed the bureaucratic process, and found it wanting.

"You mean Miss Gordon's on board the Curambria again?! With Lederbeiter the steward?" David's voice was rising to fortissimo once more.

Tam interjected. "We don't know about Lederbeiter, Sir David, remember Captain Hamilton planned on firing him." He turned to Captain Clegg. "You said Miss Gordon is going back to Britain. Where will she land and how long will it take for her to get there?"

"The Curambria will stop in Boston to load more passengers then sail to the south of England, Southampton I believe. Weather permitting, it should take 12 to 14 days."

David jumped in. "Boston, you say?! How far is Boston from here and when will the Curambria arrive there?"

"They'll get there tomorrow afternoon and leave tomorrow evening. How far it is from here? It's about 250 miles, a good eight days' ride."

David's face fell, Tam however, asked "And by train?" Clegg sputtered in his beard. "I'm sorry, I have no idea. I've never been on land long enough to find out."

Fred Black, the clerk, however, was a fan of railways and had been listening to the interchange. "Pardon, sir, there are express trains running between Manhattan's Penn Station and Boston. I read that express trains average thirty miles an hour on flat ground which means it should take nearly eight hours to get to Boston from here. And most express trains leave around eight in the morning."

Clegg viewed the clerk with a new appreciation. "How do you know this, Mr. Black?"

"My uncle is a railway man and we often talk about trains, sir."

"Mmmh, good work, Mr. Black, good work. Come and see me tomorrow morning at 9, I'll find something more suited for your talents."

"Yes Sir!" Fred no longer begrudged the lost sleep!

"Captain Clegg, I have one more request. I presume you have a counterpart in Boston, an immigration officer like yourself?" Clegg nodded. "Would you please send a telegram to him and have Bella Gordon removed from the Curambria and held until I arrive? Miss Gordon's testimony will go a long way towards eradicating this stain on your organization's reputation."

Captain Clegg caught David's meaning, cooperate and I'll make sure you come out of this blameless, don't cooperate and you'll bear the consequences. He nodded with emphasis. "I take it you're leaving for Boston this morning? When you get to the Immigration office, ask for Captain LaFleur. He'll be expecting you."

"Thank you for your assistance, Captain Clegg. If there's nothing else, please excuse me, I have a train to catch."

David and Tam took their leave and made haste back to the fishing boat, woke Ronaldo and Guido and set sail for the dock at the foot of Manhattan Island. Tam paid Guido the agreed upon sum and attempted to send Ronaldo home but the agent was having none of it. "You're my responsibility until I'm relieved at seven tomorrow, rather, this morning."

The trio had to walk a long way before they found a coach stand. Even then, Tam had a tough time persuading a coachman to take them to the Waldorf-Astoria. It wasn't the money, it wasn't the distance, the smell was the problem, all three passengers stank of fish. About two in the morning, that international lubricant, money, worked its magic and a coachman agreed to take them to the hotel. David asked to be dropped off at the tradesmen's entrance at the rear in case any villains were waiting for them up front.

Once in their suite, David got down to business, stripping as he gave his orders to Tam. "First, Tam, have these clothes burned, I can't see me wearing them ever again!

Second, you'll need to meet with the Gordon's and tell them what has happened and what I'm doing in Boston. I expect to have Bella in my care by the end of tomorrow but she won't be back in time to join her family on the train to California at two. I'll get her a ticket on the earliest possible train but she won't catch them up until they get out west. Make sure you get their California address and let them know I'll send a telegram once Bella's on the train." An acute pang of sorrow flashed across David's heart at the thought of saying a final goodbye to Bella. He shook his head and continued. "Bring Jonathan up to speed too. Oh, and here's another bearer bond, please cash it tomorrow, we'll need ready money for our trip to St. Louis and Arkansas."

Tam noticed how slim the folder of bearer bonds had become. David saw his glance and laughed. "It would shock my grandfather to see how I was using my inheritance, but he would approve wholeheartedly, even if I end up spending it here in America! Meet me here at seven." He checked his timepiece, "Three hours from now, so you'd better get to it!"

#

"You look like death warmed up!" David didn't appreciate Tam's greeting when they met in the lobby of the Waldorf-Astoria the next morning. David had had little sleep that night, tossing and turning as he thought about the predicament Bella was experiencing.

"Tam, you don't seem so spry yourself." David retorted, getting a dig in at his older friend, "spry" being the code word used to describe senior citizens. "You'd better drop me off at the station before you meet the Gordons." He paused. "We should keep the worst of the news about the Lederbeiters to ourselves for the time being. No need to tell them about girls disappearing. Agreed? Very well, let's go! I suggest we take two carriages, we need room for the bodyguards too."

The two Scots squeezed into a carriage along with three of Pinkerton's men. Two more bodyguards followed in an open landau. They had not gone far when a commotion erupted ahead of them. The lead bodyguard stuck his head out of the window, sat down again and said. "There's a dray overturned in the road ahead. I'm going to assume it's planned." He pulled a whistle from his pocket, blew three quick strident notes, grabbed david, yanked him to the floor and sat on him! The other two agents were at the windows searching for attackers and the two in the landau behind ran up and jumped on the running boards of the coach. Everyone had a revolver in their hand.

David was protesting as much as one can with a beefy 250 pounder sitting on one's chest, Tam was covering as much of David and his protector as he could, a gun appearing like magic in his hand. The senior agent was screaming at the coachman to take a different route "… at once!" but the coachman saw no need for hurry, until a bullet knocked his hat off. Soon there were bullets flying everywhere. One of the agents sat down with a flash of pain and surprise on his face, gaping at his bloody hand which was now missing two fingers. Tam pulled him aside and took his place at the window, joining the Pinkerton agents who were returning fire with relish. The coachman whipped his horses into a gallop, wheeled to the right up a side street and soon the ambush disappeared behind them.

"Tam, get this ape off me and help me up!" David had seen nothing of the attack and didn't appreciate acting as seat cushion for a behemoth. David scanned the coach and spotted the injured agent. "Sir! Let me examine your hand. Tam, give me your kerchief! Tell me what happened, Tam!"

"You know this was an ambush, Mr. Rennie." A statement, not a question. "The overturned cart was to block us into one place. Sir, what's your name?" Tam asked the lead agent who had sat on David.

"Noggie O'Reilly, Mr. McKenzie." Noggie was still watching the road ahead and behind.

Tam turned back to David. "Good instincts, Mr. O'Reilly, ex-military?"

Noggie grinned and said "Yes, but not on your side!"

Tam got the point, the Brits and the Irish had been warring for centuries. "Mr. Rennie, Mr. O'Reilly here threw you on the floor and saved your life."

"Oh, that's an exaggeration, don't you think, Tam?"

Tam leant over and put two fingers through holes in the back of the carriage, just at the height of David's head. "No sir, I don't."

David was quiet for a moment. "Noggie, I'm indebted to you. I'll make sure your employer rewards you."

"No need, sir, that's my job. Anyway, I'll be making a full report to my boss."

David nodded to Tam who understood. Tam would make sure the agents would receive a bonus for their sterling work.

Noggie called up to the driver, telling him to slow, there was no sign of pursuit.

"How many were there, Noggie?"

Noggie replied, "I saw four. Would you agree Mr. McKenzie?"

"Yes, one in front, one behind and one on each side, a well- designed ambush."

"And what happened to them?" There was a cold, hard edge to David's voice even Tam had never heard.

"I got one." Tam replied. "How about you, Noggie?"

"I got one too, and I think my men got another one."

"So, one got away." David mused. "He'll report back to his boss who'll want to finish the job. Tookov is bound to have paid them well so we can expect another attack."

The coach halted outside Penn Station and David dismounted with the unscathed Pinkerton men. "Tam, make my apologies to the Gordons and let them know I plan on bringing Bella back to them, although where and when I don't know. Drop this man," he gestured to the wounded agent, "at the nearest infirmary first. I'll see you back at the hotel sometime tomorrow, all being well. Keep Jonathan informed."

Tam nodded his acknowledgement and directed his coach to the Albion Hotel. David entered the station accompanied by his guards who saw him settled into his carriage and stayed with him until the whistle blew to signal the train's departure. David's mind focused on Bella now, Tookov and his father's fortune seemed a distant fantasy, one still needing action, only not now.

Chapter 27

Is this Hell?

That was Bella's first thought as she came out of her swoon, hearing vicious hacking coughs, pitiful moans and groans and desperate shrieks for help. She cracked open an eye and peered around her, not moving her head. The ill surrounded her and they were much closer than she desired. There, within touch, was a woman of about thirty, smelling of vomit, diarrhea and garlic. Curled up into a ball, rocking back and forth, she keened loud and long. It took Bella a moment to realize she held a baby in her arms although the baby was quiet. A nurse, a Lady in White, appeared and tried to take the baby but the woman screamed even louder and refused to give up the infant. Another orderly came, a man this time, and pried her hands loose. The baby still was quiet. Then Bella realized the baby was dead. The orderlies left and the woman descended into an unresponsive calm, but still rocked and rocked. Welcome to America.

With the orderlies out of sight, Bella risked opening the other eye. She was on a wheeled gurney which gave her a vantage point to view the corridor. Most of the sick lay on the floor on stretchers and filled the hallway, almost from side to side, making it hard for the medical staff to navigate this chaotic passage. She turned her head to the other side and saw the back of her old nemesis, Lederbeiter the steward, talking to the male orderly and pointing to Bella. Lederbeiter was leaning into him, browbeating him, but the orderly, Ivor Davies, a round, powerful man with red hair and a 32" waist under a 52" belly, wasn't buying what Lederbeiter was selling. He stood there, arms folded, determination writ large on his face. "I don't care who your cousin is, I'm not releasing this girl into your charge. She's to appear before the committee tomorrow morning if she's well enough. And if she doesn't catch typhoid in the meantime." Ivor Davies left in search of new crises, a quick journey taking him a mere six feet away. Bella closed her eyes and turned her head back but the movement caught Lederbeiter's eye. "Aha, you're awake, my little sparrow!"

She felt his hand on her ankle and tried to snatch her leg away but they were in restraints! She tried to move her arms but they too were bound to the gurney. She felt Lederbeiter's hand move to her calf, opened her mouth and screamed but no one seemed to pay any attention. What was one more scream in an insane asylum such as this? His fingers moved higher, stroking her calf, sliding his hand to her knee. Her skin crawled and she screamed again, this time with no hope of being heard. But then she felt Lederbeiter's dirty paws being torn away, the orderly had heard the screams after all.

"Get your hands off this patient!"

Lederbeiter was foolish enough to take a swing at Ivor who, having grown up in Hell's Kitchen, was a much better brawler than the steward. He ducked Lederbeiter's clumsy swing and fired two quick, short, hard jabs into Lederbeiter's gut. The steward dropped like a sack of potatoes, retching for air. Ivor pulled him to his feet by his collar and marched him outside, his toes hardly touching the ground. Ivor dumped him without ceremony in the dirt. "Never show your face here again or you'll regret it, you hear!?" He shook his enormous fist in Lederbeiter's face, then turned on his heel and returned to Bella.

"I'm sorry, Miss, are you harmed?"

Bella felt like she would cry but put on a brave front and shook her head.

"How are you feeling?" This was not an innocent question, Ivor needed reassurance she had recovered and could advance to the Detention cage.

"I'm well enough, thank you, sir. But what happened? Why am I here? Where am I? Where's my ma? Why am I in restraints? …" Bella would have kept on going but the orderly held up his hand.

"I'm sorry, Miss, I'm only an orderly here and don't know much. I understand you fainted at the Inspection Desk and nurses wheeled you here to the hospital. I'm to take you to the detention pen when you recover which is fortunate for you because many of these people are suffering from typhoid and you're much better off away from here. Beyond that, I know nothing. Who was the man who had his hands on you?"

The change of subject took Bella's mind away from her questions. Ivor started to push the gurney through the stretchers on the corridor floor

"He's a rapist pig, is who he is! Please keep him away from me!"

"I'll do what I can, Miss." Ivor took pity on the young lassie. "You'll be safe up here in Detention. These bars don't only keep anarchists like you in …" (he smirked at his own joke) "but filth like him out. Here we are."

Bella was now in a cage with a dozen other women of various sorts, sizes, ages and nationalities. Ivor released her restraints and helped her off the gurney to a seat on a hard bench. "Look you, you've done nothing wrong, have you?"

Bella shook her head.

"Then tell that to the tribunal tomorrow and all will be well. Good luck!"

Chapter 28

Freda Lederbeiter Strauss was 5' 1", slim, elegant and the madam of this New York bawdy house. Always dressed in the height of fashion, her vanity was her hair, luxurious, long, blond hair teased up into a pompadour. She was the matriarch of the Lederbeiter clan here in America and she was very unhappy.

"How could you be so stupid as to get yourself fired? You had a real cushy job on board your boat, you were well taken care of and we got first pick of the innocents!"

Ex-Chief Steward Wilhelm Lederbeiter, Freda's brother, tried to get a word in sideways.

"But Sis, I think …!"

"Shut up, Wilhelm. How often have I told you not to think, you're not capable and it's clear you've strained yourself! How are we going to get fresh girls now? You know they wear out in a few months. Our customers are always after young innocents. Where are we going to find them now?"

"Sis, Herbert and I were talking …"

"Oh, now you're plotting behind my back, are you! Remember who's the brains in this outfit, and it's neither of you!" Freda's voice was at a crescendo now and she was on her tiptoes trying to glare into the eyes of her brother and cousin.

"No, it's nothing like that, Sis. I know I screwed up and Herbert and I were talking about another way to fill the rooms in your house." Wil was wheedling now and had enough practice around his sister to know it was best to let her vent then present a potential solution for her to consider. "It's all set up on the Curambria with three of my stewards. They'll continue to connive with me, for a price of course. They'll select the innocents, identify them to the initial Immigration Officer …"

Herbert interrupted. "The Ellis Island side will stay the same. My officers will mark the landing cards so the chosen girls appear in front of me. We get them into the detention cells as usual and make them disappear as usual."

Freda considered the proposal. "What do the stewards and the Immigration Inspectors want in return?" Answered before asked.

"They want access to the girls."

Freda's voice rose again. "Now you know that can't happen! My house is the premier sporting house in New York. My clientele is from the cream of society and they don't want to mix with the likes of stewards or immigration officers. The Mayor, the Chief of Police, the Governor when he's in town, they're welcome and frequent visitors. THERE … IS … NO … WAY I'll have your colleagues mixing with them!"

"We quite understand, Freda, we do. But we have a solution you'll jump at. Suppose we open a second house. This house here, your house, will stay the same with the same fresh girls and the same topnotch clientele. But we open a second house which I'll run with Herbert's help in his off-duty hours. The girls there, and here's the brilliant part, are the girls who have outlived their usefulness in your house because they've become jaded or hardened or whatever. Our stewards and immigration officers, and new customers who aren't associated with your house, will have access to these girls and will never set foot in here so there's no danger of contaminating your clientele. What do you think?"

Freda was quiet for a long moment, mulling over the implications. "You know, that's not a bad plan, not bad at all. In fact, I'm quite impressed. Let me give it more thought but if we go ahead, we'll need to start soon to make sure our supply keeps coming. In the meantime, find a suitable property. Have you thought of where you want to open? Not New York, too expensive." Herbert nodded his head. "Yes, we agree. How about New Jersey? It's close enough for you to keep your eye on us and the political climate is favorable."

Yes, thought Freda to herself, *I'll be keeping my eye on you. The biggest problem will be making sure you keep your own pants buttoned. Can't have you being your own best customers. Maybe I let you get it off the ground then I'll step in and take it over. Easy enough to get rid of you in New Jersey.*

"Well, boys," She smiled at each of them, "you surprised me, well done. I'll let you know tomorrow whether we should proceed. Now, I'd better be off to Ellis Island and get myself the new girl. A good one?"

"A cracker, wouldn't you say, Bert?"

"Oh yes, good looking and strong minded. She'll take some taming and I can't wait to be the trainer!"

"After me, Herbert, after me!"

Chapter 29

Ivor the orderly pushed the empty gurney out of sight. Bella watched what felt like her last friend in the world disappear and the enormity of her situation settled over her. She felt like crying but sensed her new companions would use any sign of weakness against her. She drew herself up to her full height, pulled her shoulders back and glared around the room, holding the stare of anyone who looked at her until they dropped their gaze.

Right! She muttered to herself. *Let's take stock. It's about six in the afternoon. It appears I'm to go before a tribunal tomorrow morning, whatever that is. I'll tell my story and I'll get out. I know where the train to California is leaving from so I'll meet my folks there and all will be well. I have money sewn into my clothes so I'll be able to get there in time.* The last thought was more hope than conclusion. *I only have to survive tonight. I'll stay awake so I'm not robbed ... or stabbed.*

Bella examined her latest companions. Four of them were tough and hardened by life. Bella had seen their ilk by the docks in Aberdeen and she had had sympathy for them then, women down on their luck and doing anything they could to survive, including beg, borrow, steal or sell themselves. But now they were close, whispering amongst themselves and eying her clothes with interest, Bella's sympathy vanished as her own survival instincts kicked in. *"Don't back down, don't show fear!"* She remembered her brother's teachings and put them to work.

There were other groups of women there. Three girls were more like her, in their late teens or early twenties. They whispered amongst themselves, also eyeing Bella. But they seemed almost warm, welcoming one of their own perhaps. Bella listened to their conversation and found the three had something in common, they had expected to be met off the boat by a relative who hadn't shown. The missing kinfolk appeared to be a father, an uncle and a fiancé. The girls weren't permitted to travel on their own for fear for their safety. Nor could they prove they wouldn't become wards of the state and were being held until their family appeared or until the next boat of the right shipping line showed up to take them back to the port of origin. There were a few family groupings too. As the day drew to a close, Bella identified them as having children with low intelligence. These families were in severe shock, going 'home' but nowhere to go to and nothing to return to.

The tough bunch, led by Morag Harrison, were whispering amongst themselves. "Look at her coat, it's much warmer than mine!' "And how about those boots, I'm sure they keep her feet dry!" "Where does she keep her money, sewn into a seam, I'll bet!" They sidled closer. Bella kept her defiant glare but quaked on the inside. She looked around for help but the three young lassies wouldn't meet her eye, perhaps they had been through this assault themselves.

The hard cases were almost within touching distance when the door to the detention room opened and an immigration officer poked his head into the room. He took in the scene and surmised what was happening. “Hey, you, Harrison, leave her alone or I’ll make it a lot worse for you!”

“Oh, how are you going to do that, fat boy?!” Morag Harrison had nothing to lose and men in authority didn’t impress her.

But the officer had dealt with her kind for years and knew just what would impress her. “I’ll remove you from here and put you in the infirmary with the typhoid cases if you don’t behave!” Morag fell silent and moved away from Bella, her three cohorts following. She glared at the officer, then Bella, before sitting back on the original bench.

The officer stared at Bella again, giving her the slow, appraising onceover Bella had come to loathe. “Here’s company for you, Miss Gordon.” He opened the door wider and ushered in one of the biggest women Bella had ever seen. She was well over six feet tall and on the high side of 250 pounds but it wasn’t pounds of fat, it was muscle developed from hard work. Her sunburnt skin, dotted with freckles, matched her long auburn hair. However, a dullness behind her eyes, an open mouth and a slack jaw suggested limited intelligence. She was of an age with Bella and dressed in the long brown cloak and headscarf favored by the west of Scotland women. The officer pointed and the newcomer crossed the room to sit beside Bella.

“What do you mean, ‘company’?” Bella asked but the officer smirked at her and closed the door behind him.

“What’s your name?” Bella asked.

"Catriona, Miss, Catriona McKay." The big woman's reply was slow and halting as though simple questions were a struggle. The big surprise, though, was in Catriona's voice. It sounded like a child, high, squeaky and innocent. Morag Harrison and her pals had been listening and laughed when they heard the child speaking for the woman. Catriona cast a peek at them, no anger, no embarrassment, no … nothing. Bella's heart went out to her. "Pay them no attention, Catriona, they're only being cruel. Tell me, why are you here?"

Catriona struggled to find an answer. After a while, she gave up. "I don't know."

Bella sighed, she'd hoped Catriona's story might shed light on her own situation. "Did you come to America with your family?"

Again, much hesitation, then a great outburst as though floodgates had been opened. "I don't want to go to America! I want to stay home with my ma!" Catriona stood up and bashed her head against the wall again and again, now screaming at the top of her little girl voice. The other residents of the Detention Room tried to put as much distance between them as possible, even Harrison and her comrades shrank into a corner.

Bella stood up and put her arms around the broken-hearted lassie.

"There, there, it'll be fine, you'll be going back to see your Ma, you'll return to Scotland soon, I'm sure!" Bella wasn't sure but why else would Catriona be in the Detention Room?

No sooner had Catriona's outburst started than it subsided and she and Bella sat down again, Bella holding her hand and cooing soothing whispers in her ear.

Catriona calmed, then turned to Bella. "Will you be my friend?"

"Of course I will!" She glared at Harrison and her gang. Having this giant as a friend would keep her safe tonight, she surmised.

Two hours passed and Bella found out more about Catriona, how her brothers had come to America, leaving their parents, but taking Catriona with them against her wishes. The brothers understood Catriona's size and strength would be invaluable for any work they found. But it didn't take long for the Ellis Island Immigration Officer to find Catriona's limitations and chalk-mark her lapel with an 'X' for "Mental Defect". Her brothers had debated long and hard and decided they would continue to their destination in Kansas. As Catriona didn't want to be in America anyway, they would let the Immigration folk return her to their parents. They had given Catriona a little money which she still possessed. Perhaps the Morag Harrisons of the world didn't want to risk messing with such a fine physical specimen, limited intelligence or not.

Immigration Officers brought Bella and Catriona a plate of food which looked a little like stewed prunes over dry bread. Bella didn't think she would eat the mess but ended up wolfing it down with relish. When was the last time she had eaten? Breakfast this morning? Was that this morning? It seemed like a decade ago. There was also this long yellow thing which she'd never seen in Scotland. However, after watching the other detainees, she peeled, ate and enjoyed her first banana. Catriona was enchanted!

An hour later, the lights went out and Bella and Catriona climbed into their bunks, canvas cots with a blanket. Bella chose the top bunk, Catriona on the bottom, Bella figuring if the Harrison gang were planning to meddle with her, having to climb over Catriona would dissuade them. The guards woke them at first light, given more prunes and bread and then they waited, and waited and waited. Around mid-morning, officers came and collected one of the waiting young women. She didn't return. Bella's imagination saw her being released into the arms of her fiancé and sent off to her destination, happy at last. About an hour later, one of the 'hard' women disappeared. Bella allowed a dose of spite to creep into her sunny disposition and hoped the hard case had gone back to the place she had escaped from. And so it continued, approximately every hour an officer would come and collect one of the inmates in the detention cage. Sometimes, two officers would add to their company by bringing in someone from the inspection gates. Often, the newcomers would be indignant and blustering, proclaiming their innocence, fitness or wealth. But after the officers had left, their bravado would subside and they would find a seat and stare at the floor, hoping for divine inspiration perhaps, sensing a bleak future if they didn't get the decision reversed. The atmosphere in the room was somber, even the children sat quiet as mice, most times beside their ma. Catriona kept close to Bella, content in her own world.

About lunchtime, (another banana), Bella realized she was wouldn't appear before the tribunal in time to catch up with her folks before the train left for California. *Well, there's nothing I can do about it so no sense in getting myself all worked up. I'll just take it one day at a time and deal with tomorrow when it comes, because it doesn't look like I'll be going anywhere today.*

However, about seven in the evening, the Immigration Officer opened the door again and beckoned both Bella and Catriona. "Your lucky day, ladies!" (Bella doubted that, based on what she had experienced of late.) "Come with me." They left the Detention Room, ignoring the catcalls from the remainders of the Harrison group.

They ended up in a room much more comfortable than anything else Bella had seen on Ellis Island. Furnished like the drawing room of a country house, it boasted plush easy chairs, bookcases packed with leather bound books, coffee tables with lamps shedding soft light around the room. There were two occupants, an Immigration Officer in his regulation uniform and an attractive lady about to enter middle-age. It was obvious from his uniform, his demeanor, and the way their guide deferred to him, the Officer was a senior member of the force. But it was the woman who held Bella's attention. She was tiny, barely five feet tall but held herself well and projected an air of competence and confidence. She was elegant in a light gray dress and complementing jacket. The white lace at her throat matched the lace on her saucy little bonnet. The tiny pink roses on her hat and on her lapel added enough color to relieve any monotony.

"Ah, Miss Gordon, Miss McKay, I have good news for you both!" It was the senior Immigration Officer. "First, I need to see your papers." He held out his hand, Bella and

Catriona handed over their papers. "Thank you." He glanced at the papers, then to the elegant lady and gave a slight nod. "Miss McKay, you first. I understand you'd rather be at home in Scotland with your parents. Well, I'm putting you on a ship tonight which will take you back to Glasgow. I wish you 'God speed' and good fortune."

Catriona peered at Bella, confusion evident on her face. Bella comforted her. "It's what you wanted, Catriona, you're going back to your ma!"

Catriona thought about this for a minute, then a grin spread across her face and she picked Bella up in a bear hug and spun her around in delight. "Stop, stop, Catriona!" Bella was laughing herself now, believing she might receive good news too.

The Immigration Officer spoke. "This is the first time I've ever seen someone overjoyed to be turned back! Miss McKay, please go with this gentleman, he'll get you safe on board your ship. It's called the Curambria, by the way. He'll take your papers." Only the elegant lady saw the papers being switched. Catriona hugged Bella again, a bone-crunching experience, and left with the officer.

"Miss Gordon, allow me to introduce Mrs. Strauss from the Immigrant's Aid Society. Her Society assists immigrants, like you, whose journey has been interrupted by mistake. I'll release you into her custody and she'll help you find your family."

Mrs. Strauss smiled at Bella while thinking "*The boys are right, she is a beauty. I can make a lot of money off her!"*

Bella couldn't absorb everything. Two minutes ago, she was in a detention cell, now she had this stylish lady helping her. Despite her best intentions not to be disappointed again, her heart rose. Maybe she could catch up with her family. And Sir David.

Chapter 30

Cossetted by the plush seating and drained from the previous day's and night's exertions, David reflected on the highs and lows of the past 48 hours. He had saved Bella on the ship, arrived in New York (only yesterday?), met with Jonathan, survived the attack on the carriage. He had also endured the news of Bella being turned back, visited Ellis Island by fishing boat and been bitterly disappointed to find Bella was already on her way back to Britain, it all took its toll on his emotions. And he was short on sleep, even though he was a young fit male in his prime. David fell dead to the world, not wakening for several hours and when he did, he found himself face to face with a fascinated eight-year-old schoolgirl.

"Why does your nose make a funny sound?"

"Emily!" scolded the governess, at least, she looked like one. "Hush!"

"But it sounds like a foghorn. Why?"

David couldn't help but laugh. "It does, doesn't it? It's to keep crocodiles from crawling up my nose while I sleep."

"But there are no crocodiles here!"

"See, it works well!"

Even the governess had to giggle, although giggling was against union rules. “Come, Emily, gather your things, we’re almost at our station.”

The train slowed and stopped. “Goodbye, Mr. Foghorn!”

“Goodbye, Miss Emily!”

Emily and her governess descended from the carriage and left for places unknown.

David’s thoughts turned to his favorite subject, Bella. He drifted off into a wistful reverie, interspersed with more dozing so he soon couldn’t tell one from the other. The train ride took far too long, even though it was an express with limited stops. He couldn’t wait to see her.

He took a hansom cab to the US Immigration Office in the Port of Boston, shivering in the cold autumn air. It felt like he was back in Scotland, the dampness, humidity and raw wind was no stranger. Paradoxically, he also felt more alien here than he had in New York and found himself wishing for Tam’s presence, not for reasons of safety but for companionship. But as he arrived at the Immigration Building, he shook off his melancholy and jumped out of the cab and strode into the building searching for Captain LaFleur. There was a spring in his step and a smile on his face as he anticipated meeting Bella once again.

The Captain kept him waiting a few minutes, then asked David to join him in his overstuffed office. This too had a forest of files and windows so dirty David had a hard time seeing the infamous harbor. Captain LaFleur avoided enquiring whether David wanted tea.

"Sir, thank you for seeing me at such short notice but the matter is pressing."

"Ah yes, 'The Matter'! Captain Clegg was, of necessity, brief in his telegram. Perhaps you'd be so kind as to give me the background. While I have complied with his request and removed Miss Gordon from the Curambria, her future is my responsibility, mine and mine alone." LaFleur didn't see himself as being obstructionist, it was his job to make sure he followed the laws of the land to the letter. David didn't see it the same way and swallowed hard, reminding himself achieving his goal was more important than asserting his rights, as he perceived them. He launched into the story of Bella's background, her experiences on the Curambria with Steward Lederbeiter, how Inspector Lederbeiter refused her entry to the United States, his midnight arrival at Ellis Island and Captain Clegg's assistance in finding Bella's papers.

"Ah yes, Miss Gordon's papers. She has new papers seeing she was turned back." LaFleur passed them over to David who read them in detail.

"Yes. That's her." He let out a sigh of relief. He'd been attempting, and failing, to dampen his hopes for fear of being disappointed.

"You tell a fantastic story, but so fantastic, it could only be true! Very well, Sir David, I'll release her to your custody on the understanding you will reunite her with her family at the first possible moment. Do I have your word?"

“Yes, Captain LaFleur, you have my word.” David didn’t know how to make that happen but didn’t see the harm in agreeing, he had Bella’s interests at heart. Didn’t he?

The Immigration Officer spoke into a box on his desk. “Please have Miss Gordon brought in.”

David could no longer hide his excitement and stood to face the door and greet his love. The door creaked open, too slow it seemed, and an immigration officer entered bringing … someone who definitely was not Bella Gordon!

David turned on LaFleur. “What’s the meaning of this? Do you mock me, sir? Who is this woman?”

“This woman”, Catriona McKay, stood unconcerned by the commotion she had caused, placid, content.

LaFleur became defensive. “What do you mean, ‘Who is this woman!’? She’s Bella Gordon! You have her papers in your hand!”

“You’re right, I have Bella Gordon’s papers, but she isn’t Bella Gordon!” David turned to Catriona. “Who are you?”

David was shouting by now and Catriona scooted backwards and broke into tears. Her high-pitched little girl keening, LaFleur’s angry protestations and David’s attempts to question the girl guaranteed bedlam which got worse until David got a hold of himself. “Quiet, everyone, quiet please!” Peace reigned and the three caught their breath.

“Miss, I apologize but I need to know who you are.”

Silence.

David was about to raise his voice again when he realized Catriona's limited ability to comprehend. "Miss, I apologize for my outburst. Won't you have a seat?" David was speaking as to a child now, slow, soft, trying to calm Catriona's fears. "Can you tell me your name?"

"Catriona McKay, sir." The child's voice seemed more incongruous.

"And can you tell me where you got these papers?" David pointed to the Bella Gordon papers on Captain LaFleur's desk.

Catriona glanced at the papers, shook her head and bawled. "I don't want to go to America! I want to be home with my ma!"

The young woman's outburst took the men by surprise, but confirmed their understanding of why Catriona was a returnee.

"Was there anyone else with you when you left New York?"

More silence, more hesitation, more confusion showing in Catriona's eyes. "I left my friend there."

"Who's your friend, Catriona, do you remember her name?"

"Bella!"

“Ah!” A collective sigh of relief. David sat back in the chair he had appropriated. “Thank you, Catriona, thank you! Now, tell me, please, did Bella get on the ship with you?” David thought the error in the paperwork might lie at the feet of the Curambria’s crew.

More thinking, more silence until... “No, she stayed in the nice room with the comfy furniture.”

Captain LaFleur spoke. “I know which room she means. It’s used by the Immigration management to meet or entertain outside visitors. Tell me, my dear, do you remember the name of the Immigration Officer in the room?”

The wheels of memory ground slowly and painfully, as was evident from Catriona’s face. At last she spoke again. “No, but the pretty lady had pink roses in her hat!”

David and LaFleur looked at each other, perplexed, then David understood. “There was a lady in the room with you? Catriona nodded.

“Anyone else?”

Catriona shook her head in the negative.

“Can you tell me anything else about the lady?”

More deep thought. “She was small, she only came up to here.” Catriona pointed to her chest. Another pause. “And she dressed well.”

“What happened to Bella? How was she? Was she all right?”

Catriona retreated from David's barrage of questions and lapsed into silence. David cursed his eagerness and waited until Catriona had calmed.

"Bella's a good friend, isn't she?"

Catriona came back to the land of cooperation. "Yes, she's a good friend."

"Pretty, too." A statement, not a question.

"Yes, pretty too. Pretty grey eyes."

David glanced at the Captain. "That's her, she has the most amazing…" He caught himself. "That's her. Catriona, do you know what happened to Bella?"

Catriona seemed perplexed by the question, as if it was something she should know but couldn't remember. She got upset again and began to bawl, wrapping her arms around her body, trying to shrink into the smallest human being she could be. No coaxing from David or LaFleur could pry anything more out of her.

"Well, Mr. Rennie, it would appear your journey was for naught."

"Yes and no, Captain LaFleur, yes and no. At least we know Bella's not on the Curambria. Captain Clegg will help me identify which of his officers was in the plush sitting room and I'll question the officer when I get back. Somehow, I feel the key lies in identifying the woman he was dealing with. I'll be able to find out more about her. I feel sure she'll know something."

"What about Catriona?" LaFleur nodded to her, still dwarfing the too small chair.

"She's an innocent bystander, don't you agree? She wants to go back to her ma, why don't you let her?"

"I agree, and, if we hurry, we can get her back on the Curambria. And you, sir, if you hurry, can catch the overnight train back to New York! Good luck, I trust you find your Miss Gordon safe and in good health!"

Chapter 31

David got little to no rest on his way back to New York. He tossed and turned in his sleeping berth, fretting over what to do next, what he should have done, which Lederbeiter to strangle first. He caught himself several times but Tam's admonishments regarding the uselessness of worrying worked only for a short time. It was a long night but David made it back to the Waldorf-Astoria in time to catch Tam having breakfast with Jonathan and George, Bella's brother.

"Gentlemen, how are you? George, I didn't expect to see you here. I thought you'd be on the train to California."

"Good morning, Sir David, I'm here to escort Bella. Where is she?"

David slumped into a chair, close to defeat. "The truth is, I don't know." David swallowed hard. "She wasn't on the ship, they had substituted someone else. My best guess is she's still in New York, perhaps still on Ellis Island."

There was a stunned silence, then Jonathan asked for more details so David recounted his meeting with Captain LaFleur.

Jonathan stroked his mustache. "I agree with you David, she probably is still on the island. What's your plan?"

"I need to find out who the elegant lady is, she's the key. I'll go back to Ellis Island and get Captain Clegg to find the Immigration chappie who was in the plush room with her and follow up from there."

Jonathan smiled. "Can I save you some time, David? Use the telephone!"

"What? The telephone? I've never used one. Is Ellis Island linked to the hotel?"

"Only one way to find out. Waiter! Ask the concierge to join us please, as soon as possible. Thank you!"

The concierge materialized at Jonathan's side and confirmed David could telephone Ellis Island from the hotel. He offered the services of one of his young porters who was the hotel 'expert' in the new technology. David accepted and the two disappeared to a booth in the lobby. Jonathan, George and Tam took more coffee and toast, attempting to keep a normal conversation going but it was stilted at best. George was working himself up into a towering rage when David returned a half hour later. He appeared stricken, pale of face, sweating, sad, confused, determined and furious.

"What is it, David?"

"They've taken her to a brothel!"

George leapt to his feet. "A brothel? What do you mean, Sir David? My sister in a brothel?!"

Tam grabbed George's arm and pulled him down to his seat again. George wanted to punch anyone who glanced at him sideways.

"David, please tell us what happened. You got Captain Clegg on the phone ..."

David sighed. "Yes, I told him about my trip to Boston, how a switch had been made and how the real Bella Gordon wasn't on the Curambria. I asked him about an immigration officer meeting with an elegant woman in a plush drawing room. He recognized at once where I was talking about and had a good idea who the officer was. Captain Clegg called the officer, or rather, ex-officer onto the carpet and browbeat him until he told him everything, how Ellis Island Officers kidnap attractive young ladies by switching them with someone who was rejected and heading back to Europe. This racket has been going for two years and fills the ranks of prostitutes for the 'elegant lady's' bawdy house. And she has protection from on high, the Chief of Police is a regular. Her name, by the way ..." David's anger almost boiled over, but, with a great effort, he controlled himself. "Her name is Freda Strauss, Freda Lederbeiter Strauss!"

The table gasped. "Of the Steward and Inspector Lederbeiter family?" Jonathan was quick.

"The very same." David drew a deep breath. "Now, I know the address of the bawdy house. The question now is how we rescue her?" He paused. "The police?" he asked Jonathan.

Jonathan shook his head. "No, David, not in this instance. The New York police are fine, in their own way, but they also have a reputation for being corrupt and this business would attract their basest instincts. Tam, how do you feel about a private raid?" Jonathan had 'the look' in his eye. Adventure called, devil-may-care came running.

Tam perked up. "I'd like that a lot, Mr. Moncrieff! George, are you in?"

"Try and stop me. How many more of us will we need?"

David replied. "We have to assume there will be four men at the brothel, the two Lederbeiter cousins and perhaps two regular bouncers. So, we four …" David stared down Tam's protest. "… and maybe one more. Is Noggie still on watch? We can't involve the Pinkerton men because what we're doing is illegal. Noggie might like to earn a little something on the side, though."

Tam rose from his chair. "I'll talk to him. I suggest we get going as soon as possible before wind of your telephone call reaches the Lederbeiters. What happened to the officer in the drawing room?"

"For once, I'm ahead of you Tam. He's being kept in isolation until I call Captain Clegg again. He's in with the typhoid patients!" David gave a grim smile. "Serves him right." Sympathy was in short supply this morning. Tam left to talk to Noggie.

Jonathan excused himself. "I have to go back to the Consulate, I'm meeting the lady from Immigration who was on the Curambria with you, Ethel Watson? I expect I'll be back here in an hour. Will you have enough time?"

"Yes, we will. We have to make sure we have a plan, we can't just burst in, you know!"

"Why not!?" Jonathan left at his usual nonchalant pace.

#

Tam returned with Noggie and the three other Pinkerton men, including Guido, their guide from last night. Noggie preempted David's protest. "Our brief, Mr. Rennie, is to keep you unharmed. Your plan's legality is immaterial. You hired Pinkerton to see to your safety, and so we will." His sweep of his hand included all his men.

David nodded his agreement and led his crew up to his suite where the Pinkerton men goggled at the opulence and took a second look at 'Mr. Rennie'. "Right, Tam and George, you have the floor!"

The two soldiers leant on Noggin's expertise in getting the lay of the land. He said, "I know the place, Tam, I've escorted Pinkerton clients there. There are four stories. The main floor has a lounge area, dining room, kitchen and bathroom. The upper three floors are the same, three bedrooms and a bathroom. There's a basement too."

"Is there an exit out the back?

"Yes, Tam, through the kitchen. It leads to an alleyway."

“Thanks, Noggie. How about staff? Large gentlemen like bouncers?”

“Last time I was there, which was in July, there were two bouncers who were also the doormen. There were several older women servants who kept a low profile, and then the owner, who you know about. She sits behind a desk most of the time, on the right as you enter.”

“We have to assume the cousins will still be there, so there will be four men and the owner. Are the bouncers armed?”

“No, Mr. Rennie, they are huge men and being armed will seem unnecessary to them, though they may have blackjacks. I don’t see the cousins being armed, they’re not the type. However, the owner might be. She might have a pistol in her desk.”

“Mmmh, good point Noggie. Tam? George? Any suggestions?”

Tam and George conferred for a moment with much nodding of heads. Tam reported back to the group. “It needn’t be anything too subtle, Mr. Rennie. One of us knocks on the door, Jonathan perhaps, while the rest of us keep out of sight. Jonathan distracts the doorman, the rest of us break cover and rush the door. We dispatch the two bouncers and the cousins. Mr. Rennie keeps a sharp eye on the owner. If she goes for her gun, he deals with her. I suggest you two Pinkerton men come in the back way at the same time. Listen for Noggie’s whistle”

Jonathan arrived then, bringing a surprise with him, Ethel Watson of the Immigration Department.

"Miss Watson! Why are you here?"

Miss Watson drew herself up to her full height. "This is the piece wanting from my report. What happens to the missing girls? I need to see for myself and I persuaded Mr. Moncreiff here to take me along. I trust I won't be an inconvenience?" Her spine might have been steel but butter wouldn't have melted in her mouth.

Jonathan shrugged his shoulders as if to say, *You see what she's like, I couldn't refuse!* "Miss Watson brings another benefit, David, we need a woman to restrain Mrs. Strauss after we're in control of the house."

Miss Watson added "And what are you going to do with the other girls? I understand your intention is to rescue Bella, which I agree with wholeheartedly, but what about the rest of them, are you going to leave them to the Lederbeiters? Don't forget there are families still looking for them too."

"You make a good point, Miss Watson. Does the Immigration Department have any places where these girls can go for help?"

"No, but there are legitimate Immigrant Aid Societies who will. I can take care of them once they're out of the house."

"Very well. My intention is, first, to rescue Bella, and second, to give the other girls a way out of the game, and in doing so put the Lederbeiters out of business. Any damage to their premises would also be fine by me. Who has a gun?"

Everyone raised their hand, including, to David's surprise, Miss Watson. "Don't fire them unless you have to. We don't want to get the police involved. But feel free to wave them around to intimidate the opposition. Right, if there's nothing else, let's go."

#

Tam, with George as aide, positioned the men with care. First, the two Pinkerton men took their places in the alleyway behind the brownstone. "First house on the corner, this is it." Nothing like storming into the wrong house to ruin one's day. "All right, one blast from Noggie's whistle and charge in, making as much noise as possible. Guns on safety but visible. Put the fear of the devil in them! Got it?"

The two agents nodded, Guido was the senior man, steady, dependable and delighted to be a part of this illegal enterprise.

Tam and George rejoined the other five, David, Jonathan, Miss Watson, Noggie and another Pinkerton. They were around the corner from the bawdy house, out of sight.

"We're set, Mr. Rennie. Jonathan, it's up to you now."

Jonathan grinned his light-hearted grin that David guessed hid a multitude of emotions. "Right, here comes the performance of a lifetime." And he sauntered around the corner, unsteady, weaving, and hauled himself up the steps using the iron railings to help him, singing to himself. Another drunk.

Tam was crouching low with an eye around the corner, reporting back to the other four.

"He's reached the bottom of the steps."

"He's at the door now."

"He's knocking."

"He's swaying a little."

"Now he's talking to someone."

"He's going in! Let's go!" And the five avengers raced to the steps of the sporting house. George was running flat out but David sprinted past him as though George had feet of clay. They flew up the steps and threw their shoulders into the door just before it closed, knocking the bouncer flat on his back. Noggie ran in, blew his whistle, then sat on bouncer number one, his gun jammed in the bouncer's neck. Tam raced in next, stopped inside the threshold and took stock, saw bouncer number two poking his head out of the kitchen and ran to deal with him. David spotted Mrs. Strauss at her large desk on the right as Noggie had foretold. She reacted fast and was reaching into her desk drawer and picking up the telephone handset at the same time but David launched himself over the desk and knocked her to the floor. Miss Watson, last because of the long dress she of need wore, arrived in time to set a chair over her and sit on it. Chief Steward Lederbeiter, ex, that is, made a grievous error in judgment and showed his face. George saw him, grabbed him and bashed his nose to a pulp on the banister.

"Where's Bella?" Bash. "Where's Bella?" Bash. However, George was overzealous and Lederbeiter passed out cold before he could answer. George dropped him, told the final Pinkerton to watch him and raced upstairs, hard on David's heels.

"Bella, Bella, where are you?" George shouted. Neither he nor David waited for a reply and burst into the bedrooms leading off the landing. No Bella but screams from the girls inside. It was still only eleven in the morning so no customers had arrived for the lunch hour rush. "If you want to get out of here, get dressed and go downstairs!" It took the women a few moments to understand, then a whirlwind ensued as they rushed to pack their meagre personal belongings. George and David rushed upstairs to the next floor and repeated the process, still no Bella but lots of activity as the women got ready to leave. Up to the third floor, same again, no Bella, lots of packing. George and David looked at each other in despair. Then David remembered Noggie's description of the house. "She's down in the basement!" David was still in the lead and they flew down the stairs three at a time. As they passed through the parlor, David gave a fleeting glance and saw it was secure. Miss Watson was sitting on Mrs. Strauss, one bouncer still on the floor with a gun to his head, the other one recovering from being thrown around by Tam. Wil Lederbeiter was still out cold from George's pounding but where was his cousin? Horrifying possibilities flew through David's mind and he doubled his efforts to find her. He beat George to the basement door and galloped downstairs, but found four closed doors.

"Bella!" shouted David. "Where are you?" Both he and George were trying to open doors but found them locked. A muffled scream came from the second door on the right and the broad shoulders of the two desperate men splintered it to shreds. David and George stumbled over the wreckage only to stop short. Bella was there, right enough, sitting upright on a cast iron bed, hair disheveled, blouse ripped, but so was the other Lederbeiter, kneeling behind Bella, using her as a buffer … and he was holding a knife to Bella's throat. Bella's eyes flashed with anger, not fear. *Brave girl!* Thought David.

"Back off or she dies!" Herbert Lederbeiter roared, eyes wild, terror in plain sight, desperation in every action. He was cornered and even more lethal because of it.

David and George stopped their charge. David nodded to one side of the bed. George inched his way in one direction while David edged the other way. Lederbeiter's eyes darted from one to the other. "What are you doing?! Stand still! I'll kill her!" He jabbed his knife into the side of Bella's neck. She bit her lip but refused to cry out. Her eyes were on David, willing him to finish this, now if not sooner. David nodded again. George took a quick step to the side of the bed which made Lederbeiter swing Bella round as a shield. But in doing so, he exposed his flank to David. David took one quick step too, raising his arm and bringing it down with his full force, the hidden gun hitting Lederbeiter square on the temple. He dropped like a stone, the knife falling to the floor, out of harm's way. Bella jumped into David's arms, her poise vanishing as she sobbed and sobbed and sobbed, the pent-up emotions of the past days and weeks flooding over her.

Chapter 32

At last, Bella regained her composure but David kept his arms around her. George watched this with mixed emotions, David was, he remembered, one of them, the landed gentry and so deserving of George's suspicion. But George had also seen David's genuine and frantic concern for Bella, so he couldn't be all bad. George decided to keep an eye on David but cut him some slack too. Meanwhile, he had his sister to concern him.

"Are you all right, my dear?"

"I will be. No harm done, thanks to both of you! But how did you find me? Where's Ma and Da? What are you doing here, George, shouldn't you be on the train to California?" And once again, the questions kept tumbling out.

"I'll answer all your questions in good time, my dear." David was reluctant to let her out of his arms. "Let's get you upstairs and out of here. George, can you tie this scum to something solid so he doesn't go anywhere?"

Bella spoke up, surprising both David and George. "There's a set of handcuffs in the drawer." She pointed to the dresser by the bed.

The implication soared over David's head but George, the ex-soldier, recognized the significance and kicked the recovering Lederbeiter hard, got the handcuffs and used them to secure Herbert to the bed. George had murder on his mind but David didn't give him time to act out his impulses.

"Right, let's go upstairs."

The noise in the main floor lounge was deafening, Freda Lederbeiter Strauss screaming, her bouncers groaning, the servants crying, the recently rescued women and girls shouting.

"Quiet! Please! Everyone!"

At least the girls piped down but the Mrs. Strauss kept up her wailing. "Oh, put a sock in it." Miss Watson stuffed a napkin in Mrs. Strauss' all-too open mouth.

"We need to control these people. I believe handcuffs are available?"

The girls nodded their heads and rushed off to fetch them. They took immense pleasure in locking up the Lederbeiters and the bouncers, making sure the cuffs were tight and painful.

"Well done, everyone. We've met our goal of rescuing Miss Gordon. This is she!"

Bella colored and dipped a curtsy. Her rescuers applauded her and glared at the Lederbeiters.

David addressed the servants. "I plan on shutting this house down and I regret you will be out of work. Stay here until we're done and I'll compensate you. Noggie? You and your men take these apologies for human beings to the dining room, I need to confer with the women." Noggie and his men hustled the apologies out of the parlor.

David turned to the women. "This is Miss Watson of the Immigration Department." Several young women drew back in fear of being deported.

Miss Watson spoke. "You have nothing to worry about, ladies, you are safe now and won't have to go back to Ellis Island, that's behind you. You are legal landed immigrants of the United States of America. Welcome! I'll be taking you somewhere safe today and we'll find a way to reunite you with your families." The women eyed each other, could this be true, most of them had given up hope and resigned themselves to living out their lives in this hell. But to see their family again! Could it be possible?! The atmosphere lifted and became almost festive.

David got down to business again. "Where's the safe?"

The leader of the kidnapped women, a striking redhead from County Sligo called Maureen said. "It's in the desk, and I know where the key is." She darted into the dining room, strode over to Mrs. Strauss, ripped open the collar of her gown and pulled out a key on a long gold chain. One swift, strong tug and Maureen had the key and chain in her hand. The chain burned a furrow into Mrs. Strauss's neck, leaving her scarred for life.

David unlocked the small safe and found it stuffed with gold coins, dollar bills, even jewelry. "Here, Maureen, take these jewels and distribute them amongst the girls. Let them pick one at a time and there won't be any squabbling.

Make it quick. Tam, take the money and divide it in half. Take one half and share it amongst the girls. Give our brothers here..." he motioned to the Pinkerton men, careful not to mention names "a handsome fee for their trouble. Make sure the servants get something too."

It took but a few minutes for Tam to divide the Lederbeiters' stash.

"Noggie, bring the Lederbeiters and their pals back in here. Oh, and have them bring Miss Gordon's cabin trunk up from the basement. It's outside the second door on the right. Ladies, you have five minutes to pack what you want. Miss Watson has telephoned for cabs and will take you away from here. If you want to leave your imprint on this place, like breaking a mirror or suchlike, be my guest. You men," the Pinkertons, "feel free to help. I don't want this place to be habitable when we leave!" Mrs. Strauss heard David's last command and struggled harder to speak but the gag stopped her from being heard. The Pinkertons broke everything in sight, furniture, mirrors, plates, glasses, bottles. They pulled curtains from the walls and smashed chandeliers. The women hurried upstairs to wreak as much damage as possible. "Noggie here will blow his whistle when it's time for you to go. George, please bring Inspector Lederbeiter up to join his family. I want him alive and in one piece, hear me?!" George sped off.

Meanwhile, Tam, was standing near 'his' bouncer who was still cowering in the corner, licking his wounds so to speak. Tam was watching David, in command, clear, decisive, confident and every inch the man. *His father would be proud of him.* This random thought surprised Tam. His normal thoughts regarding Lord Rennie were rarely positive but also it reminded Tam there were bigger issues at stake, like catching Baron Tookov. *"Time for Tookov later," he thought, "let's tie up the loose ends and get out of here."*

Noggie grabbed David's arm. "The five minutes are up and I would like my men to be out of here as soon as possible. The longer we stay, the greater the chances of someone coming."

"I agree, blow your whistle, Noggie."

The three groups assembled at the foot of the ornate stairs which were made of wrought iron and impervious to assault. The kidnapped girls were irrepressible, chattering like a barrel of monkeys, the Pinkertons laughing amongst themselves, enjoying the chance to be destructive, David and his group eager to leave.

"We need to get out of here now. What do we do with this lot?" David nodded to the Lederbeiters and the bouncers.

"Slit their throats!" shouted one young, demure, ladylike Scot.

"No, I won't allow murder or maiming. Nor can we set fire to the building, there are families on this side to consider."

Maureen interrupted him. "I have an idea; will you trust me to act within your rules and carry out a just punishment? Pleeease!?"

David hesitated, then remembered what Bella had endured, in fact what all the girls had endured. The Lederbeiters and their gang deserved whatever punishment the girls came up with. It might even help the girls in their healing from their ordeals. "Very well, though no fires, no murder and no more injury!"

"Yes sir! Now, you must wait outside! Bella, Miss Watson, come with us, please."

The Pinkerton men set up lookout posts outside. David, Tam and George stood in the street wondering what Maureen had in mind. They didn't have to wait long. The front door opened and Maureen came out. "I give you the Lederbeiters!" And out they came, one by one, prodded by the women, the bouncers first, then the cousins, then Mrs. Strauss, head down, still handcuffed … and in their underwear! The Pinkerton agents jeered, passersby joined in, soon the whole assembly was laughing and pointing and the Lederbeiter group were getting more and more embarrassed. The bouncers were in their red long johns, the ones with a flap on their behind, while the male Lederbeiter's long johns were gray, they might have been white at one point. But Mrs. Strauss, ah, Mrs. Strauss! What a sight! A black and pink corset, black stockings and high heeled shoes! And bald! Maureen had run clippers all over Mrs. Strauss's head, removing any trace of her beloved pompadour! Maureen had made sure the handcuffs kept everybody's hands behind their backs so there was no covering up the spicy parts. The Lederbeiter group gazed about them wondering how to get away from this torment and found nowhere to hide. "Off you go now, be on your way!" and with much kicking and cursing, the Lederbeiter group shambled up the street, no clothes, no money, no position in society any more. Maureen flourished the key to the house, locked the door and slipped it into her dress.

"Brilliant, Maureen!" laughed David. "A perfect revenge!"

"Thank you, kind sir! Thank you! I suppose I'll never know your name. I asked your lady in there but she wouldn't tell me. Thank you for rescuing us and for setting us up with the means to find our families." She grabbed David by the shoulders, leaned in and gave him a huge kiss and hug. "Here, take this." And she pushed her hand into David's jacket pocket, beamed at him again, and left. The other women repeated the hugs with David getting redder by the minute. While he was being embraced by the bloodthirsty Scottish lass, he could see Bella grinning at him over the lassie's shoulder which gave him a smidgeon of relief.

Within minutes, Miss Watson had herded the women into the carriages and said her goodbyes to David and the Gordons. Jonathan left with her to lend his official weight to Miss Watson's negotiations with the real Immigrant Aid Societies. Two Pinkerton men loaded Bella's trunk onto David's cabriolet and joined the other Pinkertons as they followed David and his group back towards the Waldorf-Astoria. David and Bella sat side by side facing the front, facing their chaperones, Tam and George noticed the young couple were holding hands but thought it was appropriate after what they had been through. However, Tam had been thinking ahead.

"George, what are your plans?"

George jumped as though he had woken from a hundred-year nap. “I don’t know, Tam, I haven’t had time to plan anything yet. What time is it?” He answered his own question by pulling out his pocket watch. “It’s not yet midday! I thought it was much later.” The wheels turned in his head and he called up to the coachman. “How far is the railway station from the hotel?”

“Twenty minutes, half an hour at the most, depending on the traffic, sir.”

“And the train to California left at two yesterday. Sir David, do we have time to swing by the hotel and pick up my luggage?”

David’s answer was a long time in coming, he didn’t want to let go of the hand he was holding so soon. In the end, he put logic before emotion. “I believe so.” He heard Bella gasp as the reality of the situation became clear.

“Very well, let’s go to the hotel first, then the station. Thanks to you, Sir David, we have enough money to buy tickets many times over.” He was getting excited now, the prospect of catching up with his parents and starting a new life in California.

“Sir David, perhaps George and I should get another cab, go back to the hotel, get him packed and checked out. May I suggest you and Miss Gordon stay in this carriage, drive around the park, and meet us at the station. Let’s not forget Baron Tookov’s Sicilians.”

David shook himself as though to clear his head. “Good point, Tam. George, agreed?”

“Tam told me of Baron Tookov and his hired hands. What he suggests is sound. Can I trust you with my sister?” Both David and Bella came out of their seats in protest before they saw George’s gentle mocking smile. “Weel, under the circumstances, I’ll let you off this once! You seem to have my sister’s best interests at heart!” The carriage burst into laughter.

Chapter 33

Central Park was busy at this time of day, riders getting their exercise, carriages of innumerable shapes and sizes pulled by horses or pushed by nannies, even a few infernal combustion engine automobiles. The leaves were swirling off the trees creating a multihued carpet of oranges and reds and golds but it was clear autumn was past its best. The sky had clouded over and a brisk wind was whipping the coats of the women scurrying for shelter. The men held onto their hats with one hand and their furled umbrellas with the other, leaning into the gusts to keep their balance. David and Bella saw none of that. Their eyes were on each other, a mixture of relief and anguish, excitement and despair.

David broke the silence at last. "I have so much to explain and so many questions to ask and I don't know where to start. Help me!" He smiled and Bella's heart somersaulted, again.

"I know what you mean! I'm still trying to understand what has happened since I got on the Curambria. And how you always seem to turn up at the right time to save me. How can I ever thank you?"

"No thanks are needed, Bella. It's been a tumultuous journey for both of us. Attacks on you, attacks on me …"

"Attacks on you? What do you mean?" Bella was holding both his hands now, her eyes searching David's face with concern.

David realized Bella knew nothing of his quest or the Tookovs or the Sicilians. Or the attack in Glasgow and the two attempts on his life here in New York. Or the mine in Arkansas.

"Let me tell you why I'm in America. My father was defrauded by a swindler called Baron Tookov from Russia, more accurately known as Peter Thomas from London. Father invested everything he had in a mine in Arkansas, but it now seems likely there's no value to it, no value at all. However, my family's only chance to recover some money is for me to examine the mine and, if possible, beard Tookov." He spent the next five minutes describing his travels, downplaying the mugging in Glasgow and the knife and gun fights here in New York.

"When will you be leaving for Arkansas?"

"I need to see Jonathan Moncrieff again, the fellow from the Consulate, and the Pinkerton people. I expect I'll leave for Chicago the day after tomorrow and transfer to a train bound for St. Louis the next Day."

"This is all the time we have?" Her voice was breaking. "Can't you come to California with me?

Logic and Passion perched on David's shoulders and whispered in his ears.

"Say you will, David. Go with her. Follow your heart and embrace this good fortune that has been laid at your feet." Passion seemed so…logical.

"David, don't listen to him. You have responsibilities to your family. You can't just walk away from them. They need you. You gave your word. IT IS YOUR DUTY!"

David sighed, looked up at Bella and squeezed her hand. Duty before love. He'd seen it a hundred times at home. Friends or neighbors deeply in love but married off to someone else for economic or political reasons. Logic was right. He had to choose reason over passion. He groaned.

"Yes, my dear, it would seem this is our only time together. I have to put my family first in case there's an infinitesimal chance of saving the estate. But I swear to you. Whenever this is over, whether I succeed or not, I will find you as soon as I can."

Bella drew back, crossed her arms under her breasts and looked out the window to break the spell of his hypnotic gaze. "David, I can't bear the thought of losing you." She smothered a sob. "Promise me you'll look for me! Promise!"

"Bella, my dearie." David touched his fingers to Bella's cheek and turned her head so he could gaze into her grey eyes again. "I promise you on all I hold dear. I will find you in San Francisco once my business with Tookov is finished. I can't tell you when that will be, there are too many unknowns. But I'll find you"

It seemed the most natural thing in the world for their heads to inch towards each other, a slow, tender procession until their lips touched, gentle, warm lips, their arms sliding into place around each other. Bella would forever remember her first kiss, the softness, the taste, the texture, but most of all the impact it had on her heart! David too would never forget the delicate feel of her lips on his. His heart was telling him he had recently finished a mile sprint, and he wanted so much more. His arms pulled her to him, embracing her as much as he could within the confines of the carriage.

They broke for air, grinning at each other as though, like all those new to love, they had invented something marvelous. The outside world mattered not a speck, all that existed was in this carriage, here, now and forevermore.

"David, I'll have bruises tomorrow morning! Whatever is in your jacket pocket?"

David chuckled. "I know what you mean, me too. I've no idea what this is." He took a small velvet bag out of his pocket. "What's this? Oh, Maureen must have put it there as she was leaving. It has "Tiffany" on the bag. Why don't you open it?"

Bella loosened the drawstring and tipped the contents into her hand. They gasped in unison. It was a pendant, but not just any pendant. Shaped like a shield, it was about two inches long centered by a black opal which looked like it was on fire. Blue and pink and purple and green 'flames' shot through the stone making it come alive and dance. The gold filigree setting appeared to be ringed by semi-precious stones, green garnets perhaps. It was the most beautiful thing they had ever seen … present company excepted, of course!

The pair examined the pendant for a long time, each lost in their thoughts. It was Bella's turn to break the silence.

"David, why did you take the Lederbeiter's money and the jewelry and destroy their building?"

David sighed, thought for a while then answered. "I was so angry with them for what they had done to you, and to the other women and girls before now. I wanted to kill them. Then I realized that wouldn't help you, so I thought about what I could do to make it difficult for them to start again in the same business. I decided I would destroy their building and take their assets if I could. It only seemed fair those of you who had suffered at their hands should share in the contents of the safe. Maureen's plan to strip them of their dignity was icing on the cake. I expect they'll recover but it will take them a long time and spare many a young girl. Am I a thief? I suppose I am and I'd do it again in an instant. In fact, I'd give everything I have if I could have spared you your ordeals."

This seemed a good time for them to renew their kissing, again starting with slow, soft nibbles but increasing in urgency until David pulled back, gasping for air, attempting to restrain himself. Bella thought he had made the wrong decision.

"Bella, will you take this pendant as a reminder of me. I trust we will be together in the near future but soon there'll be an awful lot of time and space between us. Remember I love you and will forever." David slipped the pendant over Bella's head.

Bella adjusted the locket so it rested between her breasts. "I understand, but, please, find me. Until you do, write to me! I love you too!"

They said no more and resumed their new favorite pastime, kissing. All too soon, their coachman knocked on the roof of the cabriolet and announced their arrival at the station. David spied Noggie and his men waiting to escort them to the platform where Tam and George paced outside the railway carriage. David saw with satisfaction that Tam had spent Lederbeiter money on a sleeping compartment.

George shot David a dirty look when he saw Bella had been crying. Bella noticed, grasped her brother's arm and said "It's all right, George, it's only my reaction to the last few days. Sir David has been the perfect gentleman." *"Well, in the main!"* she thought to herself.

"Weel, if you say so, Sis. You cut it pretty fine, the trains about to leave." As if on cue, the conductor started his "All aboard!' recital. David and Bella gazed at each other, and, not quite kissed out, grabbed each other and kissed one last time. George and Tam glanced at each other as if to say, "Where's the harm?" George climbed aboard, using the steps offered by the porter.

David and Bella were distraught, hanging onto each other, searching each other's face. Before she turned to mount the steps, Bella seized David's arms, looked deep into his eyes and cried, "Find me, David, find me!"

The End

…or not!

Acknowledgements

For a long time, I've had the sense that, as a society, we're losing something crucial. Our families are spreading further and further apart, the concept of the wise elder disseminating knowledge and family history has all but disappeared. Who are we? Who and what were our forebears? Where did we come from, not just geographically but societally also? I decided I'd attempt to remedy that loss for my own family by writing my 'memoirs'.

Easier said than done!

I soon found out that starting a memoir with "I was born on a sheep farm in the Borders of Scotland…" was a sure cure for insomnia. But, as they say, "When the student is ready, the teacher will come." I spotted an item in the local newspaper about the Writing Workshops run by **June Jefferson** at The Shiloh Museum in Springdale, Arkansas. I found not only a willing and helpful group of similar 'ink-stained wretches' but an entry into the whole new sub-culture known as the writing world. At last count, June had birthed over 300 writing groups in her quest to support writing in all its forms. Thank you, June, and thank you fellow scribes in both the Shiloh Group and the spin-off group meeting in Rogers, for your support, encouragement and camaraderie.

It also didn't take me long to realize I had an awful lot to learn about writing. I wanted my family to be encouraged to read my pages, not be turned off by its unskilled appearance and content. Next stop, then, the local community college, NWACC, where my Professor, **Dr. Lindsay Hutton,** suggested I may be able to get my fiction term paper published. Moi? Published? It had never crossed my mind. Wow! A new door opened for me to enter if I dared. And I did. Thank you, Dr. Hutton, for the education and the inspiration.

About this same time, another spin-off from June's writing group took place with a few of us creating the **Mixed Nuts**, so called because of our collective psyche and our fondness for snacks. This grrrand group is led by Da**n Baxter** and we have flourished under his leadership from a really 'nice' bunch of people to a group who can take the feedback with, mostly, equanimity, recognizing the intent behind the spoken word. Thank you, Dan, and thank you fellow Nutters.

So that's what started me writing, but where did I research my subject(s)?

THE Gjennvik-Gjonvik Archives is an amazing website which has been collecting immigrant stories and 'historical ephemera' since January 1st, 2000. An excellent starting point for me as I fleshed out my concept into written word, particularly the perils of the passage itself. Thank you, Messrs. **Gjenvick and Gjonvik**. BTW, gentle reader, if you have a thirst for knowledge about your genealogy and you have ancestors who came through Ellis Island, this is a wonderful resource.

Vincent J. Cannato's book "American Passage, The History of Ellis Island" is as thorough a book as one can find on the subject. I am indebted to him for providing further insights of the processes and problems one might have encountered at Ellis Island in 1904. You are appreciated, sir.

I'm told that the best research involves getting 'boots on the ground', that is actually physically visiting your location. I had the distinct pleasure of visiting Ellis Island some 10 years ago and was haunted by the ghosts and spirits that still haunt the halls. May I doff my hat in celebration of everyone who came through here.

Finally, Stephen King says a writer's greatest research tool is the Internet, so my thanks to **Al Gore** for creating it!

Doug Godsman

PS "Highland Justice" is the first book in a trilogy. The second book is half-written and will be finished in time for Christmas…I'm just not sure which Christmas!

DG

Jan 2018

Made in USA - Crawfordsville, IN
64633_9781981186396
02.04.2020 1523